DEATH AN
GARDENᴇᴋ

Also by Georgi Gospodinov

Time Shelter
The Physics of Sorrow
The Story Smuggler
And Other Stories
Natural Novel

DEATH AND THE GARDENER

Georgi Gospodinov

Translated from the Bulgarian
by Angela Rodel

WEIDENFELD & NICOLSON

First published in Great Britain in 2025 by Weidenfeld & Nicolson,
an imprint of The Orion Publishing Group Ltd
Carmelite House, 50 Victoria Embankment
London EC4Y 0DZ

An Hachette UK Company

Frist published in Bulgarian as *Gradinaryat I Smurtta* by Janet 45

The authorised representative in the EEA is Hachette Ireland,
8 Castlecourt Centre, Dublin 15, D15 YF6A, Ireland
(email: info@hbgi.ie)

1 3 5 7 9 10 8 6 4 2

A CIP catalogue record for this book is
available from the British Library.

ISBN (Hardback) 978 1 3996 3102 0
ISBN (TPB) 978 1 3996 3103 7
ISBN (Ebook) 978 1 3996 3105 1
ISBN (Audio) 978 1 3996 3106 8

Typeset by Input Data Services Ltd, Bridgwater, Somerset

Printed in Great Britain by Clays Ltd, Elcograf, S.p.A.

MIX
Paper | Supporting
responsible forestry
FSC® C104740

www.weidenfeldandnicolson.co.uk
www.orionbooks.co.uk

[to come]

A story, even one that happened to us personally, ceases to belong to us when it passes through language, when it clothes itself in words. Then, it is already as much from the realm of the real as from fiction.

Epigraphs

Death is a cherry tree that ripens without you.
Gaustine, 'Botanics and Immortality'

Paradise must consist of the stopping of pain.
Lars Gustafsson *The Death of a Beekeeper* (translated from
the Swedish by Janet Swaffar and Guntram Webber)

He worked the land
He now lies beneath . . .
Anonymous epitaphs for emergent occasions

Every angel is terrifying.
Rainer Maria Rilke, *Duino Elegies*

There's nothing to fear.
My father

I

My father was a gardener. Now he's a garden.

I don't know where to begin. Let that be the beginning.

Yes, we're talking about an end, of course, but where does the end begin?

I think I wet myself, my father said on the threshold. He was standing in the frame of the front door, painfully thin, slightly hunched, with that slouch typical of tall people. He had been driven to Sofia late in the evening at the very end of November. He had travelled three hundred kilometres in the back seat, lying down, to dull the pain. I had managed to make an appointment for medical tests the next day.

I wet myself, he said again, guilty like a child, apologetic and with that characteristic self-irony of his, *I've become a laughing stock in my old age.*

Everything's fine, I said, and we set about changing his clothes in the hallway, shutting the door to the living room.

I'm afraid, my daughter whispered into my ear at one point. Looking back now, I realise she was the first to sense it. I still didn't know, I didn't want to know.

*

Let me say right away that at the end of this book, the main character dies. Actually, not even at the end, but in the middle, although he will come alive again after that point in all the stories I will tell about him. Because, as Gaustine always says, in the past, time does not flow in a single direction.

When I was little, I would choose only books written in the first person from the library, because I knew that the main character wouldn't die in them.

OK, fine, this book is written in the first person, even though it's real main character does die.

Only the storytellers survive, but they, too, will die one day.

Only the stories survive.

And the garden, which my father had planted before he died.

Surely this is why we tell stories. To create another parallel corridor where the world and everything in it are in their rightful places. To divert the story down another furrow when danger and death floods in, just as he would divert the water into another row in his garden.

I would like there to be light, soft afternoon light in these pages. This is not a book about death, but rather about sorrow for a life that is ending. There's a difference. Sorrow not just for the honeycomb full of honey, but an even greater sorrow for the empty cells within it. Sorrow for that honeycomb, which the wax candles also remember, while they burn down in our hands. *Nothing to fear*, as he always liked to say.

2

The notebook I'm now writing in (I've been writing in notebooks for thirty years) was begun in October, in all innocence. He was already in pain. The signs were there, in plain sight, only the decoding came too late. I was heading off somewhere again. This time for Cracow or Frankfurt, I can't remember.

OK, but when you get back, come visit for a bit, so you can rest for a few days.

It was a monstrously intense year with countless trips. *Come visit for a bit, so you can rest* . . . I didn't pay much attention back then. He was always grumbling that we didn't visit often enough, that we didn't give ourselves any breaks. Now I read something new into those words. *Come visit for a bit*, I heard, *and stay with me, so we can spend some time together; I won't be here for much longer, I don't know whether I'll last the winter.*

*

That very October, when we saw each other for one day, shortly before I took off, standing next to the last roses of autumn:

You know, I've been having some funny pains in my lower back.

Your lower back?
And they're kind of creeping upwards.
Up to where?
Up to my shoulders. And my chest feels tight . . .

He'd gone to the doctor in the nearby town. They'd given him some pills. Whose lower back doesn't hurt these days, especially with all that working in the garden? At first, the pills helped.

I had one final trip to Portugal and then nothing for the rest of the year.

How are you, hanging in there?

Nothing to fear, he said. 'Nothing to fear' was his favourite phrase. His ready answer to every question.

Is your lower back really hurting?

Nothing to fear.

You look like you've lost weight.

Nothing to fear.

But then – I only notice it now when replaying that October over and over in my head – when we hugged goodbye, before I got in the car, he said something else.

Nothing to fear, I'll wait for you to get back.

Did I notice it then? Yes and no.

At seventy-nine he took care of a huge garden with vegetables, fruit trees and flowers. It had everything: tomatoes, peppers, potatoes, corn, strawberries, peonies, roses, tulips, trees. Planting, weeding, watering, hoeing, spraying, staking . . . We had already agreed he should stop, or at least ease up a little. I remember that then, next to those last October roses, the light purple ones, I had again told him that if he kept working in the garden like this and didn't go to the doctor he'd simply collapse all of a sudden and the garden would go to seed before his eyes. It's strange which words fate (or whatever we call that thing hidden in the future) lets into its ears. From the point of view of today, I see all the retrospective cruelty in my comment.

3

I knew that this garden was special. It had saved his life after the first cancer, it had given him seventeen years, but it would also be the death of him. It grew out of nothing in the empty yard of a village house my brother bought. *Here's where I feel my best*, he would always say. The rounds of chemo and radiation therapy had helped him, but they had also taken their toll. He never recovered his old laugh, his cheerful high spirits. He would sit in silence for long stretches, occasionally shaking his head in some soundless monologue of his own.

The garden was his other possible life, the voice unused and everything left unsaid. He would speak through it, and his words were apples, cherries, big red tomatoes. The first thing he'd do when I arrived would be to show me around. It was different every time.

I liked being there, especially in spring, burying my head amid the branches of a heavily blossoming plum tree, closing my eyes and listening to the buzzing Zen of the bees. Other times I secretly hated it, watching my father swinging his hoe, thin, stripped to the waist, revealing the scars left by operations on his sliced-up body. He and the garden became one, he wouldn't leave it, but now it, too, refused to let him go. There was some strange fatal connection, some Faustian deal, between them. I imagined it slowly sucking away his strength, feeding the fruit and roses within it – the rosier the cherries, tulips and tomatoes grew, the paler he became.

My father managed to turn every place into a garden, every house into a home. This is a particular skill. Every rented apartment we ever moved into, and we moved a lot, who knows why, always somehow become our home. For this reason now, on top of everything else, I feel homeless. I will never forget how he even managed to transport his garden with us. He would carefully dig up the hyacinth, narcissus and toadflax bulbs, the peonies and tulips – his favourite dark-blue tulips from Holland – which he refused to part with and would replant in the garden at each new place. I wonder whether flowers aren't covert assistants to the dead who lie beneath them, observing the world through the periscope of their stems.

Yes, my father was a gardener. Now he is a garden.

4

What do we talk about when we talk about death? Are we talking about the person who is absent, or about ourselves? Or are we talking about absence itself? He is so completely not here that he fills every free minute with absence.

His presence until now also reconfirmed my own presence, the presence of my childhood. Conversely, his absence sets into motion the whole machinery of memory. Things I haven't thought about in a long time are now awakening, I awaken them, so as to be sure that all of it ever existed. Voluntary and involuntary memory work together to turn the clogged mechanism of recollection, conjuring and clarifying images not clearly seen before. We must admit that this work is as much focused on the memory of the departed one as it is on us. This is the egotistical work of saving our own selves, making sense of our own remaining after someone has left.

Do we still exist if the last person who remembers us as children has passed away?

*

What do we talk about when we talk about death? About life, of course, about its whole enchanting ephemerality.

5

I call from Lisbon, noise all around me. The film festival is in full swing, and I'm on the jury, rushing from film to film. I call when there's a break between two films. *Dad, how's your back? It's fine, no big deal.* I call my mother. *Mom, how's Dad? Well, he's fine, just lying here. I'm rubbing him down with some snake venom. What's this snake venom? Well, one of the nurses' aides said it helps a lot for pain, she gave me a little.*

My father and mother lived through the pandemic. Vaccines, isolation and the village house they lived in saved them. He had already gone through cancer once, my mother had diabetes, the perfect victims for that virus. At the beginning of the pandemic I was again off somewhere else, living in Berlin for a year, so we talked on the phone every day, and I tried to catch every change in their voices: *You sound a little hoarse to me, have you still got your sense of smell, check your oxygen saturation . . .*

6

It was the end of November when he came to Sofia for tests, with a single duffle bag, a leather jacket and a walking stick. (A leather jacket, and a walking stick whittled by his own hands, this captures him to a tee). He climbed the four flights of stairs on his own, without stopping, surprising even himself. He had three more climbs left on them (and only two descents), but we didn't know that then. Every time he climbed more slowly, with more difficulty; the last time we took out a chair so he could rest on the landings between floors.

There were sixty-four steps, I counted them in my head.

I'm sure he counted them, too.

He had only a hundred and ninety-two steps left to climb.

The next day he would have a radioisotopic scan. That thing where an injected fluid settles into any areas containing 'metabolic activity' and *you light up like a Christmas tree*, as one of the doctors put it. I would quickly learn that the phrase 'metabolic activity', which sounded innocent enough, in fact most often meant tumour markers or metastases. The diagnosis was written in such a way that the patient could make sense of it if he tried. But if he decided he didn't want to know, he had that option as well.

M. in the left 4th and 9th ribs and in the right 7th rib, ill-defined growths in the liver, changes to the bone structure, degenerative and osteoarthritic changes, increased fixation of radiopharmaceuticals in the spinal column, indications of ill-defined osteolytic lesions. Some of the findings should be further investigated to rule out the possibility of . . .

Hang in there, a doctor friend of mine tells me as she pores over the test results during a short break while my father goes to the bathroom. I can sense she's trying to find something positive, some ambiguity in the brutally unambiguous test results. *There are cases*, she says, *in which things stay the same or progress very slowly, plus your dad looks like a hardy guy.*

I drove him home and went out to get something to eat. I wanted to be alone for a bit and to cry like a baby.

But there was nowhere to cry.

Some of the people on the street smiled at me, said hello, recognised me. I turned down the first side street, thank God it was nearly deserted, and there I let the tears flow. I walked to the other end, went back to the start of the street, and again down to the other end, some strange patrolling of grief. I needed to call my brother, but I didn't have the strength. I finally dialled the number, and made it brief – things weren't looking good, they needed to do more tests and that I couldn't talk at the moment – and hung up.

In these patriarchal latitudes they say that when children

cry there's nothing to fear, but when adults cry, there is something to fear. But when you're a child and an adult at the same time, and you've just found out that your father is dying . . .

The day was freezing and sunny, people were going out on their lunch breaks for a quick bite, some were walking their dogs, waving, laughing . . . The end of the world doesn't come to each of us at the same time. All of them have fathers who are still alive, I thought to myself. And then the very thought startled me. My father was also still alive.

I'll never forget one afternoon in the early eighties when my next-door neighbour was sobbing loudly in his bathroom. And his crying carried through the little open window and hung above the quiet street. He had surely shut himself up in the bathroom so that no one would hear him, but everyone did. I was ten years old and I knew something irrevocable had happened, and what is more irrevocable than death? The neighbour had just learned that his granddaughter had died, she was my age. I realised two things that afternoon: that it's not just old people who die, and that it must be very awful to have someone close to you die, if even a grown man can sob in such despair. I was at home alone, and stood petrified. I wondered whether I should go over to the neighbour's. I was afraid he'd harm himself, even though the window was far too small to jump out of, but something else, who knows? I can still hear that forlorn wail, which floated down from above like a muezzin's call in the late afternoon.

7

Every person buries their parents many times over in their imagination. That our parents will one day die is surely one of our earliest fears. *As a child I would get up in the middle of the night to check whether my mother was still breathing*, a friend once told me. This instinctive concern a child has for those without whom it would be left on its own – is it a fear for one's parents or for oneself? I'm not sure the distinction exists at that point. It's one and the same fear.

It was my first fear, too, my first recurring nightmare, my first reason to write. The dream that stalked me was simple and devastating. My father, mother and brother were all at the bottom of the village well and they would never come out. I was outside, safe but alone. Here lay my double fear: for them, and as strange as it might sound, for me, since they had abandoned me. *Why aren't we together, even if at the bottom of well?* I must have been six or seven. I immediately wanted to tell my grandma, whom I lived with at the time, about this nightmare. But she stopped me with a finger to her lips – I must stay silent, because telling such dreams out loud makes them come true, *they fill up with blood*, as she put it. But the dream kept recurring until

I couldn't stay silent any longer. So I decided to write it down. I secretly tore a page out of a notebook (I knew that writing starts from sin), and using the letters I had just learned from my grandfather I somehow managed to crookedly transcribe my dream. I've told this story before. I never had that dream again. But I've also never forgotten it. That was the price.

I sense that this nightmare, put off for fifty years, has now, with my father's death, slowly begun to fill with blood.

Writing this, I suddenly remember that my father really did go down into the well. And at exactly the time the nightmare started plaguing me. Strange, I've gone back to that dream many times, but only now has the specific incident resurfaced.

Yes, my father had to climb down into that very well to take out the pump, which was always breaking. The well was about fourteen metres deep, while the pump hung at the twelfth metre. I would stand nearby, full of fear for my father. Look, now they're tying the rope around him, tightening it around his waist and over his shoulders, he's climbing up on the rim of the wellhead. The other men are bustling around. (Why don't any of the others go down, why him of all people?) The rope is wound around the winch of the well. My father grasps the stone rim, yells *nothing to fear* (that very same *nothing to fear* he says even now, in his final days) and sinks into the darkness. The winch slowly starts to unwind, creaking horribly, which only feeds my fear. What if it can't hold his weight and breaks, my father is enormous, I imagine his body falling heavily downwards, my imagination is terrible, one, two three, metres down into the cold and dark. *Let 'er out, let 'er out*, I hear his voice as if through a funnel, *nothing to fear, let 'er out . . . stoooop.* My body is already frozen in terror, I count silently in my head. Why haven't they pulled him out yet, pull him out, pull him out . . .

Ready? the men up above yell. Aha, now you're asking, but you were all too chicken to go down there yourselves. Two terrible seconds until his answer comes. *I unhooked it, the piece of shit . . . Pull me up . . .* And the winch starts creaking again, one, two, three rotations and my father still isn't out, twelve metres is a long time, just a little more, a little more, and his curly black hair appears over the edge of the wellhead, covered in spiderwebs and bluish dust. He's alive.

Fifty years later they would once again lower my father down with ropes. This time only two metres. And once again I would be afraid they would drop him, as they lurched to one side and then straightened out again, four men whose job this is. I am six again and fifty-six all at once, but this time I have no hope.

8

This book could also start here, at Sofia airport. Actually, it could have many beginnings, only the end is always one and the same. But it is moveable, too, at least as long as we tell stories. This is my first trip since he's been gone. Now I realise that we've never actually been at the airport together, so airports shouldn't bring up memories of him. I'm supposedly here in this no man's land, a sterile zone unencumbered by the past. But he would always call me before I took off, usually after my mother, to wish me a good trip. That's enough for every airport from now on to remind me of him, making all flights different from now on.

So here I am, my first flight after my father's death is also my first trip to India. I've never flown so far to the east. My father shows up directly, with no warning. He can now travel everywhere with me, no problem, the scanners won't detect him; he waits while they check my suitcase, casually lighting up a cigarette despite the smoking bans, strolling around with that elegance of the luggage-less traveller. Now he's finally got his chance to fly, to travel; back in the day it wasn't allowed, nor did he have the money when they started allowing it, and on top of everything he would get airsick. Airports and planes become his favourite place to appear to me.

My father has also appeared to me through the faces of other people, who borrow his face or use gestures or gaits reminiscent of his. Sometimes his appearances are à la Proust, via a specific scent or taste, through the memory of the palate. On the plane to India, they serve goat's cheese with a leaf of spearmint. Specifically, spearmint, not regular mint. And with that tangy, chewed-up leaf, my father's garden unfurls across my palate – and across the palace of the sky – with its spearmint planted along the fence, ready for us to pick and put on top of sliced tomatoes, also grown in the same garden. What's more, spearmint was especially important on St George's Day to season the lamb roasting in the oven. That St George's Day, which my father bargained with the doctors for about two months earlier, asking for a deferral from God. I see him now, sitting at the table laden with the St George's Day feast, with his very own cup and his very own fork, only ever used by him, pouring the rakia, praising the salad and the crispy crust on the roasted meat, inviting us to dig in.

Thus, my father appeared to me through a leaf of spearmint, at an elevation of 40,000 feet, somewhere between Europe and Asia, in the night-time of the world.

*

On the way back, I fly through Istanbul to Sofia. An afternoon flight, the ones I love most. Now I have a particular reason to look out the window. The plane's route passes directly over the village where the house with my father and mother's garden is. I've watched those planes from down below, from that very garden. And now I can follow the monitors to see what we're flying over. I watch the sun reflecting off the river, which I know well, the dog Jacko is surely barking at the plane. If it had been before, my father would've straightened up over the rows, set down his hoe for a moment and looked up. I wonder whether this plane will also pass over the cemetery. We're flying at 38,000 feet, according to the monitor. Can souls reach this height? Or are they left to dwell down below, amid the rows of tulips and toadflax?

> There are no clouds above the clouds,
> there are no clouds above the clouds,
> just as after our death, there is no death . . .

I had written this somewhere in my early notebooks. What did I know about death back then? Later I discovered similar words in other books too. At least we are left with the consolation that we only experience our parents' death once. To say nothing of our own death. We won't experience that even once.

9

A catalogue of illnesses . . .

My father catalogued and described his illnesses just as Homer catalogued the ships in the Second Song of *The Iliad* and described the forging of Achilles' shield in the Eighteenth Song.

This book could start this way, too. When my father began listing his illnesses and injuries to the doctor, the winter morning sun was shining outside; then it started to grow dark; then it dawned again; the snow started melting; the first snowdrops appeared; the white wind began blowing (my grandfather always said – once the white wind arrives, nothing to fear, winter is over); birdsong wafted in from somewhere, the cuckoo sounding most clearly, its non-stop coos generously giving life to everyone, one year for each of its cries as the saying goes; the trees burst into leaf; Easter came and went; then St George's Day arrived . . . My father kept telling story after story, while the doctor listened at his desk, his mouth hanging open in surprise . . .

That Scheherazade – my father!

He didn't stop, earning day after day with each story, as if he knew that the moment he stopped, winter would return and he would not live to see the snowdrops or the cuckoo bird or St George's Day . . .

The doctor had simply asked whether he had any pre-existing conditions.

That was all my father needed. His whole body was inscribed with the stories of those illnesses. It was no longer a body, but rather a scroll.

Back in 195 . . ., when I was schoolboy, I broke my wrist, let me tell you how it happened . . . Then I tore my meniscus, afterwards they operated on my knee, here's the scar . . . I was supposed to play in the national basketball tournament and the coach told me . . . This incision here on my stomach is from 197 . . ., now that was a bloodbath, a whole thirty-seven stitches . . . After that they took out my spleen, it was autumn, around the grape harvest, and I could feel something wasn't quite right . . . The kids were still young then, I've got two sons . . . Then an ulcer on the duodenum, one Christmas, we'd all got together, the pig was squealing, all hell was breaking loose and . . . Then my liver, a blind biopsy . . . There was an old doctor at Alexandrovska hospital . . . His story went something like this . . . So after that I'm travelling one day and I feel this lump right here in my neck, and it's back under the knife, there was this really panicked doc, don't die, he said, on my shift, I'm begging you, so I hung on . . . Two summers ago, I'm out working in the garden, I've got roses, peppers, tomatoes, tulips, and I start feeling like everything is giving out at once, my legs, my back, I haven't got any strength, God damn it, I can barely take a breath . . .

The catalogue of his illnesses and injuries really sounded as epic as the catalogue of ships in *The Iliad*. It was even more sumptuous and vivid than the forging of Achilles' shield. These stories had everything in them – the sky, the earth, the two cities and the village with all its seasons, the reaping in the summer, the grape harvest in the autumn, the Christmas feasting in winter, with the slaughtering of the pig a whole separate chapter, told so that the blood gushed out into the office and spattered the doctor's white coat, yet the latter, absorbed in the story, didn't even flinch. Afterwards my father told stories about the garden, though he ostensibly started with the pain in his lower back while he'd been hoeing, the story blossomed into roses, cherries and plums so that the whole room began to flower. And the ultrasound sensor in the doctor's hand began budding like a tulip and there was no longer any trace of metastases.

My father kept telling tale after tale, his storytelling was a matter of life and death, he knew that if he stopped, everything he'd herded into the doctor's office would disappear like morning dew on the strawberries in his garden.

Only when he was telling stories did his ribs not pinch him, his lower back not saw him in half, his lungs not stab him; there was no trace of the pain.

Quietly the younger doctors and nurses slipped into the office. Other patients peeked in from outside the door to see what the hubbub was all about; what were these lambs and pigs, these blossoming cherry trees and stories? And whoever listened no longer felt any pain.

My father told story after story after story, and his voice disappeared slowly, and at the end, when the final sound faded, he began describing with his hands alone . . .

I'll leave him telling stories like that, because I want his novel to be light and because that's how it was. Ask the doctor if you don't believe me, in his ashtray there is still pollen from a cherry blossom and a drop of blood on the bottom hem of his coat.

10

The epicrises of language. My father's first diagnosis can be reduced to a single sentence: *Malignant soft-tissue mass with ill-defined localisation.* As they used to say in the weather forecast – expect rain showers in isolated regions. But good luck trying to figure out if you're in an isolated region or not.

The patient's external appearance does not offer any further clarity: *In degraded general condition. Afebrile. Skin and mucus membranes: pale pink. Breathing: no additional wheezing. Difficulty walking.* If you focus on the external appearance, everything's fine for the patient's age, he has a little trouble getting around but has rosy skin and is not running a temperature.

So far the medical records are still forgiving. The truth comes with the full-body PET scan. There everything is so precise, cold and unambiguous that you're left with no chance whatsoever. Only now do I find the strength to actually read, slowly and in detail, the written medical history.

Moving from top to bottom, it begins with the good news. *The scan has not detected zones of pathological activity in the cerebral structures.* (He had his wits and his memory about him until the very end.)

The scan has not detected zones of pathological activity in the head and neck.

And with that, the good news ends.

Everything below that can be summed up with a single word: carnage. It's like a description of a critically injured soldier who has been carried off the battlefield. It is astonishing how many injuries life can sustain.

Spiculated lesions 30mm in the upper lobe of the left lung. The mass has a very high level of metabolic activity reaching SUV 15.1.

Without understanding every word of this newly forged medical language, which seems to aim to simultaneously reveal and conceal, I know that things are worse than hopeless.

Idiopathic fibrosis in the upper parts of both lungs . . . Pleural-based lesion with high metabolic activity . . . Multiple lesions of varying size in both lobes of the liver up to 55mm with high met. activity, the larger ones with extensive central necrosis . . . Multiple metabolically active bone metatheses in the left femur and hip, in the right femur and hip . . . Suspected propagation in the cerebospinal canal . . .

Until now I had known that Latin was a dead language.

Now I know that it is the language of death.

Death speaks Latin.

Every description, even those just describing normal breathing or pinkish mucus membranes, still pulls you out of the ordinary ranks of the living. Language becomes a clinic. And the more detailed the description, the more marginalised the person becomes. He is no longer a person, but a patient. Here we can already see the first substitution. The objective description of your state slowly turns you into an object. The first autopsy, while you are still alive and without anaesthesia, is performed by language. It enters coldly, looks around, describes, fixes every detail and makes it visible Except that my father is no longer here. Each ever-more detailed medical description paradoxically leads to dehumanisation.

Everything is described seriously and precisely, culminating in this conclusion:

The above-described constellation of findings could tentatively be tied to primary lung carcinoma with extensive haematogenous dissemination . . . (the combination of ostensibly incompatible serum tumour markers also points to such a diagnosis), which corresponds to stages . . .

The doctor who ushers me into his office to give me the results seems like a nice enough guy, he tries to offer various alternatives, even though it's clear that they are essentially limited to local radiation therapy, which merely reduces the pain in the bone a little. I get up to leave, I want to pay for the consultation, but he adamantly refuses and with a certain bashfulness asks if I could sign a book for him, his wife is reading it at the moment, he says. I feel like asking him with all the naivety in the world, so are you going to save my father, then, and how much time does he have left, and will he be in a lot of pain, but I know there is no answer. I sign the book.

II

My father bargains for his days.

When he realised his condition was critical and that he didn't have much time left, he first was determined to make it until St George's Day. *So we can get together one last time, we've got your name to celebrate, we'll get together, have a nice meal, and then I'll be on my way, how about that?* And my father described the feast table in detail, the lamb, garlic, spearmint, it was enough to make your mouth water. For a moment, we were no longer in the hospital amid the diagnoses and metastases. The doctor started listening, too, and stopped writing in his case file. But he didn't answer the question, and my father understood. He'd asked for too much.

OK fine, St George's Day is too far away. But will the cuckoo bird at least coo for us? My father was a poet without ever even suspecting it. *When does the cuckoo sing?* the doctor asked. *Usually around the beginning of April*, my father replied. As in Balzac, he has shortened the magical shagreen of his life by a month. I thought to myself that if I'd been in his place, I would've at least haggled for springtime. The doctor just smiled and shook his head vaguely. It was as if my father was using him as a go-between to beg God for one more spring. And really, how much would it cost the Man Upstairs to give my poor old father a few more months? To look the flowers he had planted in the eye. To sit in the garden, to throw one last bone to the dog, to gather us together one last time, and then to take his leave. I'm sure he wouldn't ask for anything more than that. But God didn't seem to be listening, and his deputy here on earth, the doctor, didn't dare make any promises, either. *Well, at least till Christmas, we'll get together, see the snowdrops spring up*, my father said, looking at the doctor with such expectation. Christmas was twenty days away, almost no time at all.

Christmas might be possible, the doctor replied.

And this answer was at once the most merciful and merciless I have ever heard.

On our way out, my father stopped by the door and said: *Doc, I wanted to donate my organs, but it doesn't look like I've got anything healthy left, they're all cut out or diseased . . .*

12

Gradually everything at home takes on an order that is absolutely out of the ordinary, falling into a fragile routine. I get up in the morning and with muted fear check whether my father is still breathing. We chat about how he spent the night. On lucky nights he manages to sneak in a few hours of sleep. Then we go to the bathroom together. *Come on now, let's sit up, let's lean on our elbows, I've got you, now here's the walking stick, careful not to trip on the doorframe . . .*

With that, the most arduous part of his morning routine is completed. *Now let's fill the water bottle.* Then making something like breakfast and begging him to take at least three bites.

How about some toast?
No.
Banana?
No.
A spoonful of soup?
No.
A couple of grapes?
Let me try one.

*

The six metres to the bathroom becomes an impossible distance for him after a few days. We try a few more times – holding him around the waist, grabbing the crutch, shoving off from the bed, standing wobbly on his impossibly shrunken legs, with which he takes ant-like steps. My father, the same man who walked with giant strides and whom I had to run to keep up with.

Now that's something I will never forgive the illness for, I say to myself, I'll never forgive this. You could've taken the man without humiliating him.

I can feel his sense of guilt growing – guilt that he is sick, that he is bedridden, that he is causing trouble for others, turning their day upside down, guilt that he is a burden . . .

One of the popular myths about cancer (Sontag mentions it) is that the disease is caused by excessive repression of emotions. Although he had no way of knowing this, I heard my father admit for the first time how foolish it was that he had never hugged his own father, that that's how he had been taught, to never show his feelings, and that he'd been too strict with us, he mumbled this last part a bit . . . It was something like a small act of penance.

Please let my father not be in too much pain.
Please let my father not be in too much pain.
Please let my father not be in too much pain.
Please let my father not be in too much pain.
Please let my father not be in too much pain.
Please let my father not be in too much pain.
Please let my father not be in too much pain.

I've written this in my notebook seven times, like an amulet, that number should help. I no longer want anything else except for him not to suffer so much.

Well, we've finally come to this, the oncologist said as he wrote out the prescription for fentanyl patches.

13

Give me the mirror and let me see how I look, my father sometimes calls from the bed. I hand it to him, he brings it up close, then holds it further away. His hair is thinned, his cheeks are sunken, he is brutally skinny. I know what he'll say – I look like hell. Or I look like the Virgin Mary's holy terror. I've never fully understood that phrase, but we always laugh when he uses it.

You've got to give me a shave, he says.

What, are you going out somewhere? I reply in an awkward attempt at a joke. A daily ritual like shaving has become ever more complicated and painful, he has to sit up, propped on the pillows somehow, and that movement shifts the pain around.

I pick up a new razor, he sees me and says – *Do it with the old one, leave those be.* We lather him up, he holds the mirror, I move the razor slowly, afraid of cutting him. He grows impatient and wants to shave himself. When we're done and have wiped away the foam, he asks for the mirror again.

Well now, that's a little better, he says. And once again launches into the story about his grandfather Dinyo, whom he is named after. How, when Grandpa Dinyo was on his deathbed, his face twisted from a stroke, paralysed, pee-soaked and bewhiskered, he asked for a mirror, looked at himself and said: *Wellll, at least I'm still more handsome than that Ivan from the Zografski clan.* The Zografski's Ivan was the ugliest guy in the village.

Same goes for you, I say, *you're still more handsome than the Zografski's Ivan,* and pat his arm.

My father goes on: *With every passing year, we live better and better, but with every passing day, life gets worse and worse.* That's what one of our local fellows used to say during socialism. Funny business, that local fellow would muse, how with every passing year we live better and better, like it says in the newspaper, but every passing day keeps getting worse and worse. *That's how this business of mine is, too,* my father says now and then, attempting to smile in spite of the pain.

I look at him and think of my grandfather. Both of them worked in their gardens until the very end, until they dropped. I remember my father unsuccessfully trying to convince his father, my grandfather, to stop planting and hoeing, to rest during the worst of the heat. Once he found him collapsed in the vineyard. He picked him up, and my grandfather gave him a guilty look, like a child caught up to some mischief, and said – *Don't be mad at me, I just wanted to help a bit.* I try to convince my father in the same way, with zero chance of success.

I look at him and think: nobody has taught us how to grow old. What does one do at the end of one's life? How do you slow down, how do you get used to the fact that your job now is to rest (does resting even count as work)?

As long as there is work to be done in the garden, you exist within a protected zone, enjoying a sort of seasonal immortality. There's so much to be done just now, how could a person possibly die? Winter's the time to die, when all the work is finished.

Both my father and my grandfather died in winter, one in December, and the other in January.

14

I feed my father like a bird. Three grapes for lunch, that's
all. His bones are like a bird's, thin, sharp and fragile . . .

15

I love Epicurus, my daughter says out of the blue.

Wasn't he one of those slaves-turned-philosophers? I ask.

No, she replies, taking a certain satisfaction in correcting me, *he was the first to allow slaves and women to join his school. 'Why should I fear Death? If I am, then death is not. If Death is, then I am not,' that's what Epicurus says.*

Afterwards, again out of the blue, she comes over and gives me a quick hug: *Dad, I'm sad for grandpa, but I'm sad for you, too, because you're sad for your dad.* And then she disappears into her room.

When my daughter was born one winter seventeen years ago, my parents came immediately from their little south-eastern town to see the baby. They took the first train that afternoon and arrived the next morning. They came to our home, washed their hands and then stood in the doorway of the nursery. They had travelled on the slow camels that are Bulgarian night trains, just like the Magi. And they came bearing gifts, of course. Not exactly gold, frankincense and myrrh, although my mother had taken out the little gold earrings her own mother had given her and brought them in a little box. Along with a silver coin.

My father brought a *survachka*, a decorated branch he had made himself out of the first cornel tree; Bulgarians ritually beat one another's backs with such sticks in the New Year for good health. It was then that I realised this scene was no accident. It arose, as Borges would say, so as to re-enact another scene, another birth. I realised something else that surely every parent realises: every birth is a Nativity. A small familial Nativity.

My mother and father stood there flustered and happy, like the Magi, on the threshold of the nursery, awestruck by the baby – I'm not sure that's the right word, but it truly was an awesome feeling – though it was a tiny thing, hardly bigger than a comma, bawling and still jaundiced. They bowed their heads and did something I hadn't expected: they wanted to kiss the baby's hand. In a patriarchal culture like Bulgaria's, it's usually the other way around. The young kiss their elders' hands, the young bow and show respect. But now look how the Nativity turns everything upside down. They took timid steps forward, with such reverence, as if bowing before a person who had come from another world. (And just between us, the child really had come from another world. It had travelled nine months to get here.)

I had never seen my parents like this. Always, they were the kindest people I had ever known, but with us they didn't stand on ceremony, they certainly didn't spoil us, let alone kiss our hands. Annoying kids who should know their place, the children of socialism were loved without many rituals.

16

Exactly seventeen years ago, my father was dying for the first time . . .

A strange phrase, but I've already lived through my father's death once. The same year my daughter was born. Back then, too, my father had come to the capital city, this time on his own. That's why people come to Sofia – if a baby is born or for an emergency doctor's appointment. Some 'nastiness' as he put it, had turned up in his throat. We did the tests, got the biopsy, then I waited in the gloomy basement of the university hospital for the results. This subterranean doctor, a histologist who looked as if he had never left his cellar crammed with glass slides, took out my father's sample, shook his head and said bluntly to me: *A year, year and a half.* I remember that when I came out of that basement into the sunny and warm spring day outside, nothing was ever the same again. My father was smoking on a bench, he hadn't seen me yet. I didn't hurry to catch his eye, I stood for a short while behind the newspaper stand, I needed time to understand what I had been told. I was thirty-nine, the best thing in the world had just happened to me, my daughter, whom we had waited so many years for, had just been born. And only a few months later – my father has cancer. His final year, year and a half, began ticking down from that moment.

On that very same day seventeen years ago, when we got the little glass slide revealing his results and walked in slow silence through the city, I suggested we sit down in the botanical garden in front of the School of Journalism. We found a bench under an enormous tree, I felt it would offer us some consolation. Only then did I tell him the test results, but it was as if he already knew.

I tried to find better words, but everything sounded absurd. My head was buzzing with: *Lymphoepithelioma* (the word alone was carcinogenic) . . . *year, year and a half* . . .

No matter, he said, *I've already lived long enough, experienced the best of it, you and your brother have grown up . . . I'm not too sad about it.*

He was – let me calculate it now – sixty-three years old then. I don't recall exactly what we talked about, but it was one of those conversations you never have under any other circumstances. The disease forces out un-held conversations and delayed intimacy. Suddenly the person next to you, whom you consider invariably present, starts gleaming in his mortality, becomes translucent and fragile. The thread of his life brightens like cobwebs, which suddenly become visible in the autumn sun.

Afterwards we took a long walk home. It was only right in front of the entryway to our shabby yellow apartment block in the socialist-era prefab neighbourhood of Youth 1 that my father said: *There's only one thing I'm sad about. I wanted to live a little longer so that child will remember me, that's the only thing I want.*

So that child will remember me. That was his dream, his idea of immortality, if you will – to remain in a child's memory.

I'm losing hair by the tufts, like a whelping she-rabbit. That's what my father would say back then, after the first rounds of radiation. I wrote it down in my notebook.

And the miracle occurred, the disease everyone thought was incurable melted away. A year passed, then two and three, I counted every one of them as a gift. My daughter grew up, and my father was convinced that she had saved him.

17

At the same time, in that strange year of 2007, I received an invitation to his beloved Finland. I have always associated that country with my father, it was the first and last place he visited abroad, sometime in the seventies. A rare chance to travel to such a far-off place during socialism, though later, after 1989, he ended up never going anywhere at all. But, in the seventies, the government rewarded his agricultural collective with an excursion abroad for exceeding their grain production quotas. My father went along at the last minute, taking the place of someone else in the group who had backed out. He told stories about it for the rest of his life. Finland was made of my father's stories about it.

One member of the Bulgarian group lost his wallet on the street, my father often recalled, and the man had been distraught, to the astonishment of the Finnish police. Why are you worried? Someone will find it and turn it in, they said. And that's exactly what happened the following day, astounding the Bulgarians.

My father would also tell us how they were only allowed to exchange five dollars for personal expenses. But with five dollars you couldn't even go to a museum, let alone buy a gift for your wife. So everyone in the group, including him, brought along two bottles of Bulgarian cognac to barter with, because any kind of alcohol was a sure fire hit there and could easily be traded. A friend also taught him the trick of hiding an extra five dollars under the carpet in the hallway of the train. I should clarify that the whole trip was by train, two or three days through the Soviet Union. Just imagine the fear and anxiety every time the conductor came by. My father hated such cheap tricks with a passion. At one point he came close to turning himself in, to pulling out from under the carpet those damnable five dollars that were driving him mad with stress.

One of the other members of the group rolled up a ten-dollar bill and stuck it inside a cigarette he had emptied the tobacco out of. Then he put the cigarette back in the box. He was so happy after they got through all the inspections at the border and had disembarked in Helsinki that he reached in and lit up a random cigarette, which unfortunately happened to be the one with the money inside . . .

My father, contrary to all expectations, came back with many gifts (clearly that cognac sold for a good price, plus he saved by skipping museums and galleries). I remember two of them: a wondrous flowered dress, very seventies, which my mother wore for years until the flowers completely faded, and a magical set of six crystal glasses – not a single one of them has broken to this day. When we had guests over, he would take out the glasses and would wait, ready with his stories, for someone to ask about them or to simply exclaim, *Oh, what lovely glasses, are they from abroad?*

Anyway, when I received the invitation to go to Finland for several days, my father was still undergoing radiation, so I turned it down. But he found out and with that stern voice from my childhood told me in no uncertain terms – *There's no question about it, nothing to fear, I'll just be lying here in any case.* I thought that if, at that particular moment, I went to his beloved Finland, it might cure him.

So I went when the white nights of June had just begun. And on the very last day of my trip, at midnight (which was as bright as day), due to one careless step, I broke my ankle badly, all three bones, a triple fracture. Sorrow makes our bones brittle. I've told the story of my stay in the Finnish hospital with my broken leg and my even more broken English elsewhere. I'll only add here that magical thinking continued working within me and I recall telling myself – Who knows, perhaps this is the price I need to pay for my father to be given a little more life.

I came home (was brought home) in a wheelchair a week later and 'did my time' for the whole summer of 2007. My father lay in the kitchen, poisoned by chemotherapy, while I lay in the bedroom, with two crutches and a volume of Joyce. (There are few ways to read *Ulysses* in its entirety, unless you are laid up with a broken leg.) Meanwhile my baby daughter cried and laughed in the living room. The best and worst things have always happened to me in one and the same year.

18

During my father's first dying, he told me that he wasn't keen to keep on living. I did not quite understand that he said this to console me, so, to revive my father's keenness for life, I opened up an orange notebook with the intention of writing down everything that made life worth living. I imagined listing all sorts of things, beginning with my brother and me, his grandchildren, my mother, then moving to roasted lamb on St George's Day with mint and freshly sprouted garlic from the garden, via the Dutch tulips and first snowdrops, the silence at dusk, the cooing of the cuckoo bird in spring, to the cherry tree in June and the tomatoes in July, and so on . . . I don't recall whether I actually wrote anything down and where that notebook went. I think it stayed empty.

But when he finally got back on his feet after his operation and treatment, my father went back to the village, where he started working seriously in the garden – hoeing, planting, watering, weeding . . . The garden became a wonderland. And his keenness for life returned. He started eating again, in fact, his sense of taste first returned thanks to the peppers he grew himself and spent the entire

44

autumn roasting. That garden had everything: the old Dutch tulips that he carried with him, stately roses and peonies, geraniums, chrysanthemums, dahlias, toadflax, narcissi, white and blue violets, morning glory, calla lilies, and later the ever-growing rows of tomatoes, the furrows containing peppers, both green and red, potatoes, egg-plant, chickpeas, beans, zucchini, garlic, onions . . . All of this he planted and tended to with his two hands – but just writing it out hurts my own. Every autumn he would say – *Next spring, if I'm still alive and kicking, I'll plant this and that* . . . He would call me on the phone in the spring – *I've got one hundred and thirty-seven snowdrops, come and see them.* He always knew the exact number, as if familiar with each individual stem, he knew what had sprung up where, what was dejected, what was cheerful. *And the hyacinth is blooming as well – seventy-five blue, thirty white and eight pink, come and see them.*

I can't right now, Dad.

But the cherry tree isn't doing well this year. God willing, we'll have lots of quince.

That was the news from the world in which he lived. The world in which he wanted to live.

19

It is now a different year, and while my father and I wait for the isotope test results that will confirm the inevitable in the cold hospital hallway, I distractedly read the posters on the walls. Each one touts painkillers to ease the final phase of disease. It strikes me as arrogant. It's crystal clear why we are waiting for these test results (*scintigraphy* – even the name alone doesn't offer much hope), but the advertisements seem to know the results in advance, saying – sooner or later you'll fall back on us, we're here, write down the name just in case, so you don't have to waste time finding it later when its needed. I'm on the verge of writing the drugs' names down, in case, God forbid, we do reach that point. In the end I don't, deciding it would be a bad omen. I am slowly sliding back into *magical thinking*.

Yet despite this, I'm still trying to keep my thoughts sharp and practical. I manage to find a wheelchair while we're waiting for more results on the morning of the following day. He's already having trouble standing. He is in pain while sitting as well, but it's still a little easier. I glance around at the others waiting there, they all look to be in better shape than he is. I wonder what else can be done and repeat some incantatory phrases in my mind, that everything will be fine, that he simply overdid it working in the garden and that the pain is likely a combination of his rheumatism, achy joints, a pinched nerve and advanced osteoporosis. An orderly interrupts my incantations – she has recognised me, could she help with anything? I say that we're waiting for my father's scintigraphy results, and she squeezes his hand. *I work in Oncology here, on the sixth floor, we've got a great department, but I hope you don't need it.* A week later I'll see her again, this time in her ward . . .

One of the most difficult things about watching my dying father was the feeling of guilt over whether I was doing the best thing in each moment. When he stopped eating – should we call nurses to put him on IVs for twenty-four hours? *IVs are not recommended in a home setting*, a doctor says. So should we do it in a hospital? *Why torture him*, a senior nurse says, *this is the end, let him pass with dignity, the best thing is for you to be with him in these final hours.*

My father sensed we were considering the hospital and categorically refused to go.

*

I imagine him alone in a hospital room, jabbed full of IVs, the infrequent visits from the nurses, alone with his entire life at night under the fluorescent lights, and I decide I will stay with him until the very end. *We won't go to the hospital*, I tell him one night, *I, too, feel calmer when I'm here with you.*

I, too, feel calmer when you're here with me, I wanted to add. I had dragged a chair up to the side of the bed, far away enough not to bother him. I pretended to be reading, but actually I was watching him and simply sitting in the room with him, a compensation of sorts for all my absences perhaps. Now I can say, strange as it might sound, that sitting there with him, especially when his pain subsided a little, I would think how nice it was to be there together. Even in this situation.

20

So he can pass with dignity, that head nurse had said . . . but how? Death is merciless, my father lies in the middle of the living room, just skin and bones (in the most literal sense of the phrase). I fuss around him, feeling like an absolute neophyte in palliative care, unprepared, uninitiated. Until now, no one has ever died in my arms.

I haven't put diapers on anyone since my daughter was a baby. It was around 1.30 in the morning when we realised he could no longer stand up. I had already gone to bed, but I got up and dressed, put on my jacket and headed down to the all-night pharmacy. *Excuse me, I need to buy some diapers. What kind of diapers exactly?* The pharmacist asks drowsily. *Well, for my father, he's bedridden. OK, for adults, then. Daytime or night-time? Uhhh, give me half day, half night. How much does your father weigh?* All these questions are killing me, he can't get up out of bed, I've got no way of weighing him. *Less than eighty kilos?* She asks again, losing patience. *Definitely, I say, he might even be under sixty. We don't have any for under sixty, so I'll give you the ones for between sixty and seventy kilograms.* I go back home, and we make our first attempt to put the diapers on. With all my awkwardness and discomfiture at my father's nakedness.

The last time I'd seen him like this was fifty years ago at a city bath we used to go to. *Oof, just look at all the trouble I'm causing you*, he kept saying.

The next day my brother calls to tell me that they are renovating the bedroom at the village house to make it wheelchair accessible, he's ordered an automated, adjustable bed and so on, as if he is sure this situation will continue for quite some time. You can live at least a year with cancer, with metastases in the bones, as was my father's diagnosis – at least a month or two or three or five . . . *He's already in diapers*, I cut in quietly, *he can't get up*. I think this was the moment my brother realised how far-gone things were.

My father in diapers. That proud, (hyper)sensitive, strapping, tall, handsome and easily offended man . . . I remember how several times in my childhood he quit his job or was fired after an argument with his bosses. This was during the socialist period, and even I realised that nothing good would come of his behaviour. He would defend a fellow worker to the boss, see something unjust, hand in his own resignation, be fired, gaining a bad track record. *Do you realise that with that track record you're not going to get hired anywhere?* my mother would fume. *I'm not gonna sit there and keep quiet*, my father would reply and set out to look for a new job. I think one of the last positions he found before the fall of socialism was as a gardener and coordinator of occupational therapy at an isolated psychiatric clinic far outside the city. He tended the garden alongside the patients – the mentally ill, alcoholics, drug addicts. They planted tomatoes, cabbage, peppers, flowers. He seemed happy to me. Gardens have always been his salvation.

21

I would remind him of old stories, throwing him lifelines. We would laugh over how he managed to weasel out of the mandatory annual demonstrations on 9 September, marking the day the Red Army had rolled into Sofia in 1944. He would get a doctor's note from a dentist friend for precisely that date (*I'm not going to set foot at their demonstrations!*), then would sit out on the balcony in an old pair of trousers and take out the *chushkopek*, the pepper roaster, that wondrous culinary invention of Bulgarian socialism, and would roast the day away. He would wave from the balcony at all the folks heading to the demonstration, imitating the General Secretary of the Communist Party's specific wrist movement. It was a lovely picture – my father in his old T-shirt and old trousers, waving innocently at the neighbourhood ladies with their beehive hairdos and the neighbourhood men, dressed to the nines in the only suits they owned. Then he would greet them from the balcony once again, as they returned home with their half-wilted carnations and tattered paper flags. That same afternoon, he and my mother would set up our big cauldron behind the apartment building and cook the summer up into *lyutenitsa*, the classic Bulgarian sauce made of roasted tomatoes and peppers.

Well now, how is it that you always get a gum infection right on 9 September, the local Party secretary would ask when he called my father into his office the following day. *I can't make head or tail of it, either,* my father would reply, *my teeth are like those bourgeoisie they didn't quite manage to kill off, they're barely hanging on, and do nothing but cause me problems.*

Another afternoon, my father was varnishing the hardwood floor in the living room, having read how to do it in the book *Home Handyman*. Wearing an old gas mask he'd found somewhere so as not to poison himself with the fumes, and stripped to the waist, because it was July, he looked like a Minotaur crossed with a dishevelled soldier. Suddenly the doorbell rang, and my father, without giving it a second thought, answered it just as he was, wearing the gasmask. The postwoman screamed and took off running down the stairs. A neighbour from the apartment across the way stuck his head out and nervously asked whether they had sounded the alarms.

I can picture my father like that, in his gas mask, standing in the doorway, yet another freeze frame, another story in his fairy-tale caravan, his first-aid kit of tales.

22

Let him not be in pain, just let him not be in pain . . . I secretly pray to St George as I watch my father being knocked down more and more often in his battle with the dragon of pain. The drugs change quickly, as they too lose their battle, to be replaced by stronger ones, and when those, too, cease to help – yet others, and so on and so forth. Pain is always one step ahead.

He is not on file anywhere, he is not registered in the government's official list of cancer patients, as that would require a biopsy to show precisely what kind of carcinoma he has, and which is the primary tumour. But no one wants to do a biopsy given the state he's in, all the doctors quietly decline. Only the oncologist refuses to give up. Young and exhausted, he sees me in his tiny little office which reeks of cigarettes (yes, oncologists smoke, too); his phone rings constantly but between the various calls he writes out the prescription for the latest round of painkillers and tries to find someone to do the biopsy, calling somewhere for a PET scan. He gives me the first fentanyl patches, the weakest ones, in case the pills stop working. I didn't want to move on to patches quite yet. Once you start with them, there's no going back, you've retreated yet another level.

The great cat-and-mouse game with pain continues.

I'll take whatever you tell me to, you just dole 'em out to me, my father says. He's given up, he's left everything in my hands. We try to make some tactical moves, we alternate one set of drugs with another, I attempt to preserve the gap between one dose and the next, I put it off a bit, but then the pain attacks suddenly and we have to double the dose. Sometimes it subsides for hours at a time, but we both know it's an ambush and that we must be ready for the poisoned darts of pain. The weaker patches no longer work, so I call the oncologist two days later. I once again visit him in his smoky little room. *We don't have any of the medium-dose patches, so I'll give you the strongest ones, and you'll cut them in half. It says here that you're not supposed to cut them, but never mind.*

We've moved far beyond any warning shots or accepted protocols; every weapon at hand can be used; the fight has turned dirty. I call a friend whom I know could find marijuana without much trouble. They say it helps dull the pain, they also sell some kind of cannabis tincture. He gives me the phone number of a trusted dealer, but in the end we don't get that far.

Perhaps the only good thing about pain, I think, is that its physical swaddling hides many metaphysical abysses.

23

I walk through the city and peer into cramped courtyards;
I make the rounds of the bus stops where the old ladies
usually sit and sell the first snowdrops. If there are snowdrops, I tell myself, then my father has a chance.
There aren't any.

I read the world through the horror of this impending
death. I see in everything some hint, some double meaning.
It's as if every company has decided to advertise ointments
for lower back pain and aching bones on TV. Pain in your
lower back? No problem. Just buy a tube of this and before
you know it, you'll be out playing with your dog or skiing
in the mountains or running around the park with your
grandkids, with no trace of pain at all. I quickly change
the channel, my father smiles. Signs everywhere. Even in
the phrase *crossword* I see only *cross*.

24

My father has settled down with the newspaper they brought him this morning. Only the sick read newspapers nowadays. My father, who watches all the TV news and reads all the newspapers, gets riled up, gets angry. Why do those who are leaving this world follow its news? Is it because it brings them comfort to be able to tell themselves – I'm leaving a world that is going to hell in a handcart in any case, so why should I feel bad about it? (And the news is truly apocalyptic, in total synchronicity with our private apocalypse). Or is it that they also want to live out this world's final minutes, the everyday things that life is made of, the weft of the world, the trivia?

Or perhaps they simply hide behind the newspaper's pages, so that we cannot see their pain-twisted faces.

At the same time as my father lies dying, three hundred metres away from our home, the city's Monument to the Soviet Army is being dismantled. It took us a full thirty-five years after the fall of the Wall to get rid of it. Metal arms and heads soar in the air, dangling from cranes. The crowd's chants reach us through the open window. That regime's death is as long and ugly as its life was.

Sometimes I feel uncomfortable when I hand him the newspaper and see the headlines on the front page. Good God, what nonsense he has to read in these final days of his. I am ashamed of the world my father is dying in.

25

Newspapers and crossword puzzles. After he reads through every page in detail, my father turns to the crossword puzzle and sinks into its labyrinth. Or rather, he tries to run away from the pain through its winding corridors. You don't interest me, Mr Pain, I'm not thinking about you, I just want to remember the eight-letter name of that Dutch football player from the recent past. Or that three-letter brand of trucks. Or that French film . . .

I recall how one evening years ago, he and my mother had called me in excitement to inform me that one of the crossword puzzle's 'down' clues was the eighteen-letter title of one of my novels. *I hope you guessed right*, I joked, *now that's a true measure of success, making it into the crossword puzzles*, I laughed. I was happy that they were happy.

*

I saved several of the newspapers containing the crossword puzzles that my father worked on during his final days. This must be one of the last ones, looking at the date, it might even be the last. Partially filled in, with big letters in his clear, decisive handwriting. Two days before he died.

Public burning of heretics during the Middle Ages. A breed

of hunting dogs. A North American Indian tribe. A sad feeling,
melancholy. A former Italian footballer, from the national team.

Some of the squares have been left blank. He didn't fill in a French poet from the sixteenth century with four letters or evil creatures in the fantasy genre, again with four letters.

No one saves completed crossword puzzles, you solve them and toss them. But these are especially precious to me. I have his handwriting and his words from two days before he died. Strange what things remain at the end – *auto-da-fé, setter, Apache, sorrow, Baresi* . . .

While you're solving a crossword puzzle, death does not exist.

26

Bolka. Bolko-o. Bolchitse!
Pain. Oh Paain. Ohhh my dear little Paaain!

The shortest poem written by a Bulgarian poet, Alexander Gerov. It's got every stage of pain – from initial registration, through intolerability, to the attempt to plead with it, to tame it, to beg it for mercy . . .

During the third week I decided to read to him to keep his mind off the pain. I knew he liked the Bulgarian writer Chudomir's cheerful stories, the old edition having always been on hand at home when I was a kid. I went to the used bookshop and found that exact edition, with the red cover and illustrations by the author himself. Only they didn't have the first volume, so I bought the second. I lay down next to him and started reading aloud. I had never read to him before. I read the stories that had always made me laugh before, but now struck me as incredibly sad, perhaps because they awakened memories of reading in another, happier time.

Actually, the story itself didn't matter. I lay there next to my father and read to him, and that was enough.

The next day I saw that he had continued reading the book on his own. He showed me Chudomir's diary, which was included at the end. *He passed away in December, too,* my father said nonchalantly. Both of us felt that casually dropped 'too' left hanging in the air.

I had forgotten that Chudomir describes his final days, dying of bone cancer. In fact, he jumped out of the hospital window, unable to stand the terrible pain . . .
   Nothing to fear, my father says, seeing the expression that flashes across my face.
   Empty page???

27

I have to go to Geneva for one day; I try to turn it down. *There's no reason to turn it down, go,* my father says, *I'm here, I'll wait. Now don't you go running off anywhere,* I try to get away with a joke. He smiles. He hasn't been able to get up for several days.

I walk through the streets of Geneva at the end of November, where some sudden sun has brought crowds of people out to the shores of the lake and the Christmas market is open, the first mulled wine, cinnamon biscuits, wursts, hubbub. I know that there will be no Christmas this year. Actually, there will never be Christmas again. And I feel like crying. Here, at least, nobody recognises me.

In the evening, I have to pull myself together. I'll be receiving an award, which will make my father happy. I have to say a few words. Borges, who is lying in that very city, helps me. During the day I go to his grave. I stay there for a long time, until it starts to rain. Two crows keep me company. Borges selected a single line for his epitaph. How do you choose what will remain there at the end after so many words have been written?

I copy down in my notebook those which have since been
left upon the stone:
   And ne forhtedon na.
   Nothing to fear . . .

Borges and my father.

28

I catch myself trying to put off the most terrible part of the story, the death itself, elongating his final days, going back to his previous dying seventeen years earlier, thinking of stories in which he is alive, which took place years before the present moment. I know that we cannot skip over death. But we can at least put it off for a little while longer. Telling the story of a death is not any easier than living through it.

Everything I encounter in those final days is some kind of sign. That's how it seems to me, at least. This portentous reading comes from the portentousness of the moment, rather than what is written. I happen upon the Dirac equation of quantum entanglement, which suggests that two systems, which have a very intense and close interaction, will remain connected in a particular way. If something happens in one of the systems, the same thing or something similar happens in the other system too, even if it is thousands of miles away from the other. Consolation in case of emergency, death and separation.

One day my mother also makes an urgent trip to Sofia;

her haemoglobin is critically low. I leave my father at home and trek from hospital to hospital with her.

She is diagnosed with leukaemia.

She starts treatment.

She is sent back home to us after the first round of injections. On top of everything else, it turns out she has caught Covid.

She lies isolated in one room.

My father lies in the living room, unable to move.

My daughter, also sick with Covid, is on a cot in the bedroom.

Our home is a field hospital.

My father, who is clearly dying, greets my mother with the words: *Oof, Rada, Rada, we'll both die in Sofia, and we won't even be able to see each other.*

We all laugh at the absurdity of it all.

We're sitting in the living room one evening, my father in the middle of the room, my mother on a chair next to him. I want to ask them so many things, but can never overcome the awkwardness. I open up my notebook and say: *OK, I need your help for something I'm writing, so tell me – what games did you play as kids?* They are reluctant at first, seeing straight through my pathetic lie, but they gradually start to reminisce and for a little while (or so I'd like to think) they enter into the protected territory of their own childhoods. Where there is no dying.

I've split the page into two and on the left I've written down my father's games, and my mother's on the right.

My father:

Tip-cat, spud, buck huck, beshki (a game using pebbles instead of marbles), *blind man's buff, hide and seek, hoop-rolling, leapfrog, cops and robbers . . .*

My mother:

Pretending to cook with grass and red pepper made of ground-up bricks; pato-o (hopscotch); Chinese jump rope; dodgeball; duck, duck, goose; rag dolls . . .

Each of them played at what awaited them. And neither had a single real toy. A post-war fifties childhood. I realised that almost all these games were depicted in Pieter Bruegel the Elder's painting from 1560. Their childhood was not very different from that of four centuries ago.

I see them as a boy and a girl, he with a shaved head and patched trousers, her with short hair and a faded red skirt. And I quickly slip away into my room.

There is only childhood and death, as Gaustine always used to say.

I'm talking about childhood so as not to talk about death. Only there, in childhood, are we, for all practical purposes, immortal. In most cases.

29

You always imagine that in the final days of life you will utter the wisest words, you will leave your legacy, you will talk about the very essence of things ... But the pain sweeps away everything. Amid diapers, opioid patches, mind-numbing pills and bloodstained sheets, it is not possible to ponder the world with wisdom and grace. Sometimes I think pain – physical pain in particular – is sent to ease our separation with the world. To prevent us thinking about the most fearsome thing in those frightful hours. The pressing task is dealing with this tightness here, that tearing there, these stabbing pains in the bone marrow (they say that the pain in this stage of bone metastases is one of the most unbearable), how to dull that piercing blade. You'll say to yourself – if it's going to hurt this badly, it's better I die now, this instant. The physics of pain liberates you from the crushing emptiness and the metaphysics of death, which you are staring in the face.

My father did not groan, he gritted his teeth and tried not to be a burden. When my brother or my aunt called to ask him how he was, he would invariably reply, albeit in an ever-quieter voice: *Well now, I'm fine, I'm just lying here watching TV.*

The shrinking of life. There are different degrees of enfeeblement, of the body's surrender. Day after day parts of him give out. *I can't feel the bottom of my feet any more,* he says. *I can't feel my right leg from the knee down. My left leg . . .*

I rub and smear his arms, legs, chest, back, his sharp, jutting bones with pointless creams. We keep doing crossword puzzles. He no longer has any voice or strength.

He simply writes out the words in the air with his fingers.

What were his final words, what did he say at the very end? They'll ask me at the funeral. *I don't know,* I'll reply, and that's the honest truth. I was with him every minute of those final days, I could have made something up or seen something in his groaning that I could've wrung sense out of. But there were no final words. He just wanted us to open the window, he pointed at it. At the very end, and perhaps these were his final words – *It really hurts now, it really hurts . . .* Later, minutes or an hour before he passed, he tried to sit up and made a half-circle with his hand. Excruciating pain comes at the end, pain with which life tears itself away from life.

Actually, some of his last words that I do remember were completely practical: *Put my ID card somewhere convenient, so you'll know where it is when you need it.*

Discreet help for when the time comes to fill out his death certificate, since he knows how chaotic and distracted we are.

30

My father's first-rate stories for all sorts of situations . . . That's what I've written in my notebook, and when I open it now instead of *first-rate* I read *first-aid*. Indeed, in a certain sense first aid is precisely what they offer, appearing in an emergency, appearing like anaesthesia . . . I'll reach for them when things get tougher here. Actually, I think I'll start now.

Take this one, for instance, with all the qualities of a Fellini film, about what my father did right after he came out of major throat surgery during that first round of cancer. A rumour was going around the village that it wasn't simply an operation, but a veritable bloodbath, that they had all but sawn his head off, he only had days left to live and so on. The villagers even made one of his friends call him from the phone at the post office to check. *Well now, forgive me for asking,* the guy said, *but here folks are sayin' that they've cut your head clean off, and we don't know if you're alive, if you're gonna make it, so I told myself I may as well just check on him,* the villager said. *Hang on a second while I get my head and I'll tell you all about it,* my father replied, and the guy on the other end of the line hung up on him.

As soon as he was released from the hospital for a brief break, my father dug up an old pair of white trousers from his younger years, put on a white shirt, borrowed a white suit jacket from a friend and even found a white Borsalino somewhere. He added a sheer scarf around his neck as the final touch, to cover up the gash. And dressed like this, he got on the dusty village bus and landed in the village square, all in white like Mastroianni, right in front of the pub where the old men were drinking their mastika, the shepherds were driving the sheep home, the local busybodies were waiting to see who might turn up at the bus stop, and the kids were kicking a deflated ball around. The people, some of whom thought he had already given up the ghost, froze on the spot. *They were staring at me*, he would say, *and making the sign of the cross.* My father sat down, lit up a cigarette, drank a cognac and Coke, bought the others a round, got back on the bus, and barely made it around the bend in the road before collapsing. That's the kind of person he was.

Or this story, very different and much later. He was driving home, but on his way out of the city he found himself desperate for a pee, so he decided to stop by my brother's office and do his thing before continuing on to the village. He stopped, rang the doorbell, and was greeted by a workman, who was painting the hallway or some such thing. *Is the big boss here*, my father asked him in his typical joking way. *Uh, nope, he's gone out somewhere*, the workman replied. *I'm just gonna take a quick whiz*, my father said and did just that, traded a few more pleasantries with the workman and went to leave. At the door he suddenly realised that he had gone into the wrong entryway of the building, that there was a completely different sign outside . . . He told this story several times in his inimitable way (*so I'm thinkin' to myself – when the heck did they start these renovations, but . . .*) and we would be rolling with laughter.

31

While my father is dying, the world, of course, doesn't know and is not concerned with our personal tragedy, life goes on . . . People stop me on the street, congratulate me on recent success. I receive several invitations for events and discussions. *Don't turn them down*, my father again says, sensing my hesitation. I go. I try to pull myself together. Unexpectedly at one interview the question of fathers and childhood comes up. I feel the lump choking my throat, my voice grows thin, I take a long swig from the bottle of water on the table . . .

I have already described my father's death. Or at least, the death of the narrator's father in one of my novels, if that can pass as an alibi. The truth is that I have thought about this moment many times over the years, I have feared it, imagined it in detail. It's one of my first childhood fears, my first nightmare, the one that caused me to start writing, that dream about the village well and my whole family at the bottom of it.

The narrator in the above-mentioned novel is faced with the dilemma of whether or not to seek euthanasia for his terminally ill father, who is also progressively losing his memory. '*My father, seeming to sense this, delicately helped me. Just as parents subtly sacrifice themselves for their children their whole lives. He passed away on his own.*' In his final minutes, the narrator lights up a socialist-era Stewardess cigarette, left over from his seventies stockpiles, in his father's honour, to return him via the smoke to the time when he was young.

Now, outside the confines of any novel, while he is lying there and cannot get up, he asks for a cigarette. I hesitate for several seconds, but then go over and take one out of his pack (blue Rothmans, Stewardesses exist only in novels nowadays). I open the window, bring him a little plate for an ashtray and insist on lighting the cigarette up for him. He grasps it between his fingers, takes exactly three drags and stubs it out. I highly doubt he remembers that he is re-enacting a scene that has already been written. He continues to be the most beautiful smoker I have ever known. He was one of those people who learned to smoke from the films of the fifties and sixties. That can't be forgotten. Smoking is actually a beautiful thing. I think I started smoking to master the gesture myself, that narrowing of the eyes as you inhale, that particular choreography of the hand that holds the cigarette. He had long, beautiful fingers (albeit destroyed by manual labour), which the cigarette emphasised.

32

While my father is dying . . . That is the event. Everything else happens against this backdrop. The patriarch of the Bulgarian Orthodox Church has been urgently hospitalised, and is in the pulmonary ward, they announce on the evening news.

We know that in my father's case, everything likely began in his lungs. The patriarch is in the ICU.

Can't let him beat me to it, my father says.

All the clergy are asked to pray for the patriarch's health. Can't they pray for my father, too? I think.

The patriarch dies three months after my father. So the prayers did help to some extent, in the end.

Winter suddenly becomes a deadly season. Or perhaps you simply see what's on your mind. A writer friend is passing – Joan Acocella. We had been office neighbours during our fellowships at the New York Public Library; I'll never forget how she laid out her rug, cool as can be, and took an afternoon nap on the floor of her tiny study. A wonderful woman from the generation that was interested in everything, even in our godforsaken lands, she wrote about ballet for the *New Yorker* and was working on a book

74

about Baryshnikov. During her final days, her American family created something like a news bulletin, sending emails updating us on her condition after she suffered a serious stroke. She passed away two weeks after my father, on my birthday. I've saved the message in which her family informed us of her passing as an example of a different, much brighter attitude towards death.

Let's get together and celebrate her remarkable life.

To celebrate the life, not the death.

Twenty days after my father's death (now there's the new family chronology), Franz Beckenbauer's death was announced. He, along with Cruyff, were my father's favourites. From the time when footballers were intellectuals. Once the fan has passed away, I mused, the revered idols lose their defences and pass away as well.

33

My father died and *My father is dying* are two completely different sentences. The first is a fact, a conclusion, the second is a novel. A long story with twists and turns of hope and despair, which feed and inflame each other in turn. The oxygen of one constantly kindles the fire of the other.

Death is also a linguistic problem. The word 'dies' is short and punchy. The thudding 'd' hammers in the final nail, leaving no hope. While the howling diphthong is like a cry that trails off in that final 'z' sound, the last letter in the alphabet of life.

We are still avoiding the word. My brother and I talk on the phone every day. We haven't spoken this often in years. *We need to think about what to do when . . . What agency to call in . . . Who comes to certify . . . you know . . . What happens after . . .*

*

The last time my brother came to see my father was two days before the end. I had gone out to get more diapers. When I came back, I saw that my brother had lain down next to him, just as I had been doing to solve crossword puzzles or to read to him. There is some kind of natural solidarity that comes from within, causing you to lie down next to a sick person and join his horizontal world. You leave the uprightness of the healthy person, always looking down from above (every gaze from above is hegemonic to a greater or lesser extent), and instead make yourself the prostrate person's equal, sharing in his rejection of verticality. You join him there, where you can already catch a whiff of the heavy scent of death. We stretched out next to my father like supine sentries, to show death that we were not giving him up just yet. Or to fool death, if possible, pretending there's no one here for it, we're simply lying around talking. I imagined some invisible infusion of life from the body of the living into that of the dying.

In *Illness as Metaphor*, Susan Sontag writes about that peculiar 'politics of equivocation' that surrounds cancer diagnoses. Unlike a heart attack, for example, they are treated as something abhorrent and sinister, not to be mentioned in polite society.

There is no mythologising of the cancer patient, no romance. The gaze turns away. The illness conquers you from within, it devours you. Only your bones are left as jutting silhouettes beneath translucent skin. When it comes to tuberculosis, we can have poetry and *The Magic Mountain*, but there is no magic mountain for cancer.

I would give him his final pill for the day, leaving the next one for three o'clock in the morning and would try to doze in the next room. It was a strange sort of half-sleep, ears wide open for any sound, for any movement or soft groaning. I thought about how, despite his pain, he was trying not to let on that he could barely tolerate it. I would jump up at the slightest sound, give him painkillers and go back to bed. It was even more anxiety-inducing if it was too quiet. I would listen hard for breathing, would go check on him. Opening the door in the mornings was the worst of all; I never knew whether I would find him alive.

34

And now the most difficult part of the story begins. Let's take a deep breath and get through it together. I've prepared first-rate stories as well, in case first aid is needed. Nothing to fear.

That final night around 2 a.m. he groaned a little louder. The door was open, I jumped up. His eyes already had a different sheen to them, I can't explain it. Earlier that evening I'd been especially anxious, I'd had a bad feeling since he had vomited a little blood during the day.

Why don't you come lie down next to me, he said very quietly, *instead of constantly getting up*.

I grabbed my pillow and blanket and joined him. In agony, he turned on his side, towards me, I helped him get settled, his body no longer obeyed him at all, even the slightest stirring in bed made the pain worse. That same night we'd managed to rent a large respirator to give him oxygen. I tried to readjust the tubes in his nostrils to make his breathing easier.

He gradually stopped groaning and seemed to calm down. He rolled onto his back. The snow piled up outside made the room light. I realised that we had lain down next to each other like this when I was seven and there was a terrible hailstorm that broke the window, as thunder and lightning crashed. Now everything was silent and white, I was seeing my father off and I wanted to accompany him at least to the doorway, as far as they let the living go. I lay there next to his ravaged body, held his hand, murmuring something like: *Relax, Dad, it'll pass now, we're together, I'm here with you, nothing to fear . . .*

I fathered him like he was the son, I adopted my own father, I spoke using his words, I knew (as did he) that there was nothing to be done, that this was the final night. Night with a capital N. The longest night. I tried to imagine what a person feels during such a night, on the last night, in the final hours. And I, who believe in words, had no words. But in fact that was not important, what was important was to hold his hand, he was squeezing mine, we crossed the bridge of the night and soon we would part. For the first time I was lying beside someone who was dying. Yet I didn't find it gruesome. Where we're from, we use the phrase 'now that was pretty gruesome' in such moments, when all is inexpressibly terrifying and intolerable, some deep-seated local translation of the German *unheimlich*, I suspect. I didn't find it gruesome, this was my father, always the most beautiful man, even at that moment. I lay there and breathed with him. That's what is left at the end, a few shared inhales and exhales in the dark.

I'll continue on in a moment.

35

A week earlier he had climbed up the stairs for the last time . . . In the morning we'd had to go to the pulmonary hospital in a desperate attempt to make someone agree to biopsy his lung. My father could only get around in a wheelchair at this point. But even with the wheelchair, his pain was unbearable. We found a couch in the deserted hallway of the hospital and had him lie down there. The doctors were in some endless meeting. I finally went in to see the specialist who'd been recommended to us; he took one look at the test results and refused. *Look, you're an intelligent person, there's no reason to torture him, this is the end.* It was as if one of those rolling steel shutters that are used to secure shops in the evening had come crashing down. There's no point . . . crash, this is the end, crash, crash, crash!

A whole minute passed before I got up and left. It was as if I was expecting the doctor to take back his words, to try to do something after all. It is inhumane to tell a human being that there's no point and that it's the end. I went back to my father, who was quietly moaning on the dilapidated couch in the hallway. I didn't say anything, he glanced at me and understood. *We won't make you go out anywhere else*, I promised.

We were embarking on his final climb up the stairs to the fourth floor of our apartment building, which is old and has no elevator. Every step was pain. We barely made it up to the landing between the first and second floors. We brought an old chair down. My father sat, wearing his leather jacket and jeans for the last time, snowflakes swirling outside, an awakened winter fly creeping up the inside of the windowpane. I stood behind him so he couldn't see me. We took a break on every landing, the fourth floor seeming as far away as Black Peak on Vitosha Mountain. It took almost an hour for us to reach the top.

That's it, I'm never going to go out again, he said quietly.

And that was it.

36

Lying there next to him I started to drift off, when suddenly I was startled by the sound of wheezing, as blood gushed from his throat in a little fountain, spewing over his pyjamas and the sheets. He stared at it stunned, as if worried that he'd made a mess. I took towels and started wiping him off. He seemed angry at his own complete helplessness. *It's OK, Dad, it's OK* . . . I've always been afraid of the sight of blood, but not then, I was trying to do something without knowing exactly what should be done. So is this the end? I thought to myself. Seen from the outside, I was acting methodically and quickly, we wiped up what we could, I propped a pillow under him, gave him water, or rather wet his lips.

My mother and my wife woke up and silently joined the vigil. I suddenly worried that my daughter would wake up and come into the living room. She didn't need to see all this blood and death. We sat next to him. He looked at his watch. We grasped hands. He was bathed in cold sweat. I held his hand in the darkness and that was all I could do.

He whispered *it really hurts now*, he repeated it twice, *it really hurts* . . . If a person like him is saying that it hurts, you know it truly is the ultimate level of pain.

I'll continue on later. Right now I need a first-rate, first-aid story from my father's stockpile.

37

Here's a story about him, the hero of our childhood. We went on a summer camping trip with four or five other families, back when we were kids. Our tent turned out to be too small – there was a deficit of tents along with everything else under socialism. It was too short besides, and all two metres of my father wouldn't fit inside. *I'll sleep outside and protect you from bears*, he said. We were high up in the mountains, in a place notorious for bear sightings. He kept a serrated bread knife that my mother had brought along, who knows why, beside him, just in case. *Nothing to fear*, my father said as he arranged his sleeping bag, *I'll just cut a little slice of bread for it with this knife* (that remark was aimed at my mother), *we'll have a nice snack and drink a cup of 'Bear's Blood'* – that was the name of the cheapest and most disgustingly sweet red wine sold at the time.

In the morning, we opened up the tent flap and were flabbergasted to find my father gone. We started yelling *Daaaad, Daaaad*, but were afraid to go too far, because if the bear had devoured him it might still be lurking nearby. Thank goodness, my father soon came running out of the bushes, also scared that something had happened to us.

*

85

And yet another story from the stockpile, one that he himself loved to tell.

He was admitted to the regional hospital in Stara Zagora, this time for torn ligaments in his knee, he was limping through the hallway on crutches when a female patient stopped him. *Do you live in the town of Y., on Graf Ignatiev Street, that long apartment building number 58, in the last entryway on the seventh floor? Why yes,* my father responded in surprise, *I do live there, how did you know? Well, it's just that you do such a wonderful job of hanging out the laundry for a man, you arrange the clothes so neatly that I watch you every Sunday, I even call my husband over to watch and learn as well. We live in the building across from yours. Well now, I wished the earth would open up and swallow me,* my father would say, exaggerating the scene for full effect. *So that's what I'll be remembered and recognised for all the way up at the Stara Zagora hospital?*

38

Let's try this again. We were holding his hands, and that was the only possible conversation. He was breathing heavily, his mouth open, his eyes were open too, staring upwards. *Please let him not be in pain, just let there not be blood,* I repeated over and over in my head and gently stroked his hand. I had read that light touch comforts and soothes, supporting some final receptors in the dying person, so a kind of conversation goes on. When I glanced again at my watch, it was 3.40; he also glanced at his, perhaps he was waiting for dawn, then he dozed off for a bit, it was four o'clock, then 4.10, then 4.30. The last thing he did – he could no longer speak – was that half-circle with his hand. Was he trying to gather us to tell us something? Or did he simply want to tell us to stick together? I'll spend the rest of my life interpreting that gesture.

At five o'clock his breathing slowed, with longer intervals between breaths. Inhalation, a pause lasting a second or two or three, exhalation, a long pause, inhalation again, an even longer pause, one-two-three-four, exhalation and . . . No inhalation followed. He expired – how precise that word is – at 5.17 in the morning.

39

So. I sat there for a minute or two, then got up, my actions almost unconscious, I placed my hand on his forehead, it seemed to me that he was already beginning to grow cold, I didn't know it was possible so soon. Only the pillow under his head was still warm.

What to do next? I had to close his eyes. That's what the books say. I knew this more as a phrase 'close the deceased's eyes' or 'the living close the eyes of the dead, and the dead open the eyes of the living.'

Why does no one teach us what to do with the deaths of others?

Why does no one teach us how to die, how we should die?

I didn't scream, I didn't howl, I just let the tears quietly flow.

What happens now? I need to call my brother. No matter whom you call at 5.30 in the morning in such circumstances, they already know. My brother answered immediately, he said he'd woken up fifteen minutes earlier. And this seemed absolutely logical to me, our father was dying after all, there's no way he wouldn't sense it. He sent me the phone number of the undertaker again, though I already had it. I called. They explained that first they needed to send a doctor to confirm death, then they would step in. From then on, protocol took over. The doctor came, said good morning, glanced into the room, asked for his ID card (good thing my father had prepared it for us) and sat in the kitchen for several minutes filling out the paperwork. On the whole, the ID card was more important to him than the body of the deceased. He left, then the men from the funeral parlour showed up. We gathered up his clothes in the bag he'd arrived with a month earlier. The two undertakers lifted the body along with the sheet and headed down the stairs. I followed them with his luggage, which he would no longer need. They put him in a van, slammed the doors shut and took off. And I burst out sobbing like a child.

'Early in the morning on St Ignatius's Day, four days before Christmas, at 5.17, my father passed away.' That's what I wrote in my notebook, continuing our familial lapidary chronicles of weddings and funerals, these marginalia of muteness. Then I couldn't help myself and I added *'sorrow and pain . . .'* According to Bulgarian beliefs about St Ignatius's Day, the coming year will be defined by the *polaznik*, the first person to enter your home on that day. My father left home early in the morning, called to be just such a *polaznik* somewhere else.

40

Yet what a year it had been . . .

In May the novel I had dedicated to my mother and father won a big prize. On that London night, one of those few quickly jotted-down phrases in English was about the two of them, now quietly crying with joy in a little south-eastern town, I said. The next day several carloads of journalists arrived outside their village house; *how they found us I have no idea*, my father protested when I joked that they were becoming celebrities. Later I watched some of those broadcasts, my father showed the journalists around the garden, explaining what bloomed when and which flowers were my favourite, with all the naivety of a person who has never before found himself in front of a camera. I recall that after the third interview my parents agreed to give, I called them and half joking, half serious warned them to be careful, they were inexperienced and who knows what the reporters might trick them into saying. *We've promised to give two more interviews, then no more*, they replied, *and it's not exactly an interview anyway, we just talk and they record it*. At one point my father called me, and now he was the one complaining: *I can't get my work done, I'm three days late with the spraying thanks to these journalists, and half the garden is sitting there in need of hoeing.*

At once the happiest and saddest year. Happiness lasts only a short time, like the narcissus and toadflax that quickly bloomed and faded away that same spring. Sorrow lasts for a long time, like those stubborn weeds that choke everything and which never let up, as my father always said.

I can see him strolling around the garden, stopping by the saplings, talking to himself or talking to them, wearing my old red jacket. The one in which I once toured through all the afternoons in the world, torn from so many travels. Now it's on my father's back, a man who has not gone anywhere in the last fifty years. He walks down to the far end of the yard, his jeans hanging off his old-man-skinny legs, he stops, takes a rest, continues on to the wattle fence to see why the tulips are so slow this year, then he takes off his hat, the one I sported in Berlin. My father who would keep wearing our hand-me-down jackets, jeans, foreign travels and youth . . . I walk behind him, without letting him see me, afraid he might fall, I watch him from behind his back and it's as if I am walking behind myself. And I slow down like the tulips.

41

On the evening of that same day, one by one I close the documents and web pages full of strong non-opioid and opioid painkillers, tramadol, dextropropoxyphene, fentanyl, Dicynone. As well as Lexotan (for me). Phone numbers of private ambulance services, emergency rooms, serum-glucose IVs . . . all these went unused. In the final days and hours, the biggest decision was whether he should stay here with us or whether we should take him to a hospital.

He would be happier to be with you in these hours.

His return to the village turns out to be posthumous. Finally back with his garden and his dog, where he had wanted to be the whole time. As if the garden would have warded off death, would not have let it flourish there, either the roses would prick it, or the dog would sink its teeth right into death's fibulas.

My father would travel those three hundred kilometres back home in a hearse. When he set off for Sofia a month earlier did he sense that it would be a one-way trip? Are we given any signs, or on the contrary, are we spared by our ignorance? There, in the garden, my brother would meet him and take care of all the formalities around the funeral. My brother, who took on the entire burden of my father's post-mortem existence. The next morning, I headed there as well.

The first trip when my father wouldn't call me to ask how the roads were and to remind me to drive carefully. The first arrival at the village house without him there to meet me at the gate, take my bags and give me an awkward hug. The first time entering the garden without him giving me a tour, showing me what had blossomed, what had borne fruit, what wasn't doing well, what had been frostbitten, what he would plant when the weather got warmer.

The dog, his beloved dog, with whom he shared everything, is jumping at my feet. What can I tell him now?

Let me go back just once to see the dog, 'cause I've left him all alone.

While he worked in the garden, Jacko would wait on the other side of the fence, keeping him company. The instant my father was finished, the dog would prance at his feet carrying the ball they played with. They ate together, slept in the same bed.

Once upon a time in these parts, when the master of the house died, the news would be shared with all the animals and livestock. *The master has died, may you live* – they told the sheep and the horses. In some regions they simply blew in the oxen's ears and that was that. That's how they told them about the death, in ox-speak. One puff in the ear and everything's clear. Elsewhere, among the Western Slavs, Hristo Vakarelski writes, it was very important to also tell the bees that they now had a new master, so they would recognise him as their own and obey him. Now we had to tell Jacko the dog, who never left my father's side, Bug-Eyes the cat, whom my father took in as a little kitten and fed with a bottle, as well as the other dog, Cherry, who guarded the yard.

How do you tell a dog that his owner is no longer here?

What goes through the mind of a dog whose owner has been gone for several weeks . . .?
Where are you, I sniffed around everywhere, I promise not to jump up on the table, I'll let you nap in the afternoon, I won't eat the cat's food, I won't tug at your trouser leg, I won't catch hedgehogs in the garden, I won't pester the big dog, I won't stomp through the tulips or trample the geraniums, I won't . . . whatever you say. Just come back, stop hiding . . .

The dog is the last to accept its owner's death. And the last to forget him, as we know from Homer's *Odyssey*. The only creature who immediately recognised the hero after his twenty-year absence, without needing any proof, was Odysseus's dog. Weak and emaciated, yet waiting until the very end, it only had the strength to wag its tail – I waited for you, I didn't budge from here, now I can die.

42

As I said before, it's a strange feeling, holding someone's hand as they pass. Where do those who are passing pass on to? He went gently into that good night, contrary to *Do not go gentle into that good night* . . . I realise how beautiful that line by Dylan Thomas sounds, followed by that *Rage, rage against the dying of the light*. But my father died quietly and without raging, more in line with the Stoics, without being afraid of death, without begging for mercy, just as Zeno taught.

Though he never read Seneca, my father could have uttered his same words; I can even hear his voice: *'I shall die,' you say; you mean to say, 'I shall cease to run the risk of sickness; I shall cease to run the risk of imprisonment; I shall cease to run the risk of death.'*

When he was a child, his grandmother Kalya had gone to a Gypsy woman to have her fortune told and had brought my father along with her. And the Gypsy woman had said: *This kid here'll live to be ninety-three.* In moments of crisis, in his endless hospital stays and operations for everything and anything, my father clung to that prophesy like an amulet. *The Gypsy told me I'd live to ninety-three, there's nothing to fear. A bad penny always turns up, as the saying goes.* For a while, I believed this as well, things were easier for me that way. Actually, it was none other than Kalya, his grandmother and my great-grandmother, who lived to be exactly ninety-three. Could she have secretly swiped his fate for herself?

43

The funeral rituals seem to aim at distance and alienation, preparing the deceased for his journey and the mourners for his absence. The priest reads for a long time, a recitation of words from the Gospel, rattled off indistinctly. A bit like those warnings at the end of medication adverts. And that constant praising of God, I think as I stand there listening, instead of saying a few simple words about the person himself. Only the scent of incense from the censor numbs and consoles (perhaps this is precisely the secret reason for using it).

Many people have come, relatives and friends, as well as several of his former classmates whom I don't know, but whom I immediately feel especially close to. Surely one of them is the buddy he caught worms with down at the river to earn the chemistry teacher's mercy. People whose relatives have passed on start sending greetings to their loved ones in the beyond via my father. *You give Dad these flowers, you hear? You and he were friends, you'll run into each other. And tell him that his granddaughter's gone to college already, she's aiming high, we're fine and we remember him, OK, bye for now. This* order is placed by one of the women at the very end of the line.

Well now, they'll have a fine time tonight, one cousin whose father passed away two year ago says, *the whole gang will be back together like in the old days.*

He doesn't even look like himself, that damn disease ate him up, one of my aunts unceremoniously sobs.

He's wasted away, but to me he's still the same, the tallest, the most handsome man, my father.

44

Indeed, the rituals have not changed much since ancient times. Back then they placed the deceased's favourite horses, their servants and gold alongside them in the grave. Now people are slipping things into the coffin – sometimes openly, sometimes furtively – cigarettes, matches, biscuits. Even a shaving kit.

The day after the funeral, already back in Sofia, I call my brother. *What are you up to?* I ask. *I just brought him a coffee*, he says. For forty days after the funeral, my brother goes to the grave every morning to bring him coffee and to light up a cigarette. A strange ritual, but deep down I am thankful he's doing it.

That evening my daughter and I decide to make a family tree. The person who held all the family's living and dead in his head has just passed away, so the task seems almost impossible. But there is, I must admit, enormous comfort in doing this. Placing yourself and the deceased upon the forked offshoots of the family, in that crown of crooked branches and curling twigs, makes death seem more natural, it offers explanation and conso-lation, indeed, explanation and consolation. The tree is alive, even though so many dead are hanging from its limbs.

On the one hand are the rituals, all those practices aimed at distancing the deceased from us, hiding him down below. He is now erased from the face of the earth, literally. The grave he is placed in is outside the city or village, outside the places where the living dwell, outside life. In fact, the fundamental fear is that the dead person will come back as a vampire. And this lends a certain hypocrisy to the rituals. You don't want him to go, yet you nevertheless have to banish him, because this is what nature demands. In some places they drape towels over mirrors so the dead person will not be seen or reflected in them, and after the final breath they immediately open the window to let the soul out, so it won't be left batting up against the walls like a bird or a fly. Actually, in some regions of Bulgaria, the word for 'soul' is precisely the same as for a fly – *muha, mushka, mushiche*.

That fly – the soul.

45

When I was little, my grandma took me to a funeral with her, so I still vaguely remember that keening or 'incanting' as they called it so typical of our region. Normally, the old women from the village would chant the words in piercing voices, spinning a local epic tale about the life of the deceased and the inconsolable fate of those left behind. Without knowing the first thing about Achilles and his grieving for Patroclus or about the ancient Greek chorus that would mourn the heroes and their fate, these local women of ours, who had never even left the village, turned their sobs into *epos*. It contained a reproach towards God for taking the deceased so early or at this very moment, leaving his wife alone with young children to rear, trembling like a leaf in the dark of night. But their cries also contained a reproach towards the dead man himself, or at least that's how it sounded. Who will care for your little ones, who will hoe your garden and feed the spotted black lambs, who will tend to the cow, who will delight in the horse and the dog and so on . . .

Fifty years later, when my father passed away, the great art of keening no longer existed. We had left my mother in Sofia, as the gravity of her diagnosis prevented her from travelling. Only my two aunts, one being my father's sister, walked at the head of the procession and from time to time, some keening cry would break through their tears, a remnant of that epos.

The plot – what an ugly word – was at the very edge of the graveyard, atop a knoll, and I told myself that at least he would have a nice view of the fields, the city and the nearby Bakadzhitsi Hill. (His biggest fear about dying in Sofia was remaining there.) The day turned out to be un-expectedly sunny and warm for December, and quiet . . . Just as we were throwing clods of dirt onto the coffin, my phone rang. It was the oncologist calling to ask how my father was. *We just buried him*, I said. There were several seconds of awkward silence, in which I could only hear the wind blowing in the receiver. The late winter day was drawing towards its close, everything including that phone call seemed unreal and absurd. *We've got quite a few pain-killers left*, I said, *what should I do with them, return them? Keep them*, he replied. I admit that his answer struck me as slightly ominous. Nevertheless, this doctor was one of the few who had helped during those final days and who had tried to do something. The rest just threw up their hands; it was already too late for anything at all.

I used to like visiting the graveyards of the world when I travelled. I've been to a forested cemetery outside Berlin, to a deserted village cemetery with waist-high grass (who has deserted whom?), to graveyards in Paris, Edinburgh, Prague, Zurich and other smaller cities. I especially loved the ones where nature had already won out and conquered the headstones, where the trees had grown lushly wild, mulberries and cherries in full leaf, May snow and jasmine filling the air with their scents. There is some strange sort of triumph of life in precisely such places. As the years went on, however, I stopped visiting them.

Culture and civilisation is said to have begun with the first human burial. No animal looks after its dead. If this is the case, then the cemetery is a museum, or perhaps better yet, a mausoleum, of culture. Yes, but at the same time, the (organic) end of culture also lies somewhere there. Culture no longer has the power to care for the body laid in the ground, now nature comes on shift. It assumes guardianship of that body, of the disintegration of that flesh. Nature is the final pathoanatomist, a reductionist and deconstructionist rolled into one. We avoid thinking about what happens to the body down there below, but, in fact, it's nothing unnatural. The stone cross and the name with dates is not what preserves memory, but rather the organic nature of a cherry tree sprouted from a pit, a bush, meadow grasses, or a lizard darting about nearby are what recalls the one who lies beneath. One of the most beautiful graves I have visited in my erstwhile pilgrimage was the simple grave of Thomas Mann and his family, with its small headstone and exceptionally aromatic, melliferous grasses, which attracted a swarm of bees and beetles. Their constant buzzing made the place truly magical.

That's how I imagine the parcel of land where my father lies in the future – flowers, sweet-smelling grasses and buzzing bees, winging their way to him with the latest news from the neighbouring meadows and gardens.

46

My brother continues to visit the graveyard every morning. I call him, looking for excuses to ask him how things are there, what's going on. *It's a cemetery,* my brother replies, *what could possibly be going on?* We chat about the weather, about how it's usually windier at the far end of the graveyard. The plots around my father are starting to fill up. *So, have the flowers from the funeral wilted yet?* I ask naively; we'd brought lots of flowers, it was piled high. Unexpectedly, my brother livens up. *Actually, no, they haven't changed a bit for a few days now. The dahlias and the asters have turned out to be pretty hardy.* This makes me particularly happy, who knows why – as long as the flowers last, I tell myself, then my dad is fine, with all the conditionality of what it means to be 'fine' there.

One morning my brother calls me and says that there has been a big cold snap and the flowers haven't survived it.

I subconsciously make a list in my head of 'firsts' since my father has passed away.

The first Christmas without him. We left the table uncleared on Christmas Eve, a feast for the dead in accordance with local tradition.

The first New Year when I don't hear his voice at five past midnight.

My first trip abroad when he doesn't wish me a safe flight.

My first birthday with no phone call from him.

It appears that after every death, just as after every birth, the world begins anew. Our personal chronicles change after such events, opening up new eras. You start saying – *Ah yes, that was before my father died. Or while my father was still alive. Or two years after . . .*

That's how it was when my daughter was born. The world divided sharply in two – before the common (or the child's) era and after that.

I keep receiving emails from people who knew that my father was sick but didn't know that he had passed. 'I hope your father's health has improved considerably and that his condition has now stabilised,' they write. In a certain sense, yes, his condition has stabilised, there is nothing more stable than death.

47

I've caused you a load of trouble, my father would groan, *I'm going to ruin Christmas for you.* He so wanted to hang on until then, but there were seven or eight days to go, an impossibly long time.

My brother came for Christmas, our father already gone. We sat in the same room where he had lain and where he had breathed his last just four days earlier. It was the same people who got together every year, only the closest family. Except that a candle was burning in my father's place. *Well, he gathered us together again this year,* I said quietly, not daring to glance at the flickering flame.

So as not to be a burden on the kids. A typical phrase that could describe their whole post-war generation. In one of the final conversations with my father before all this happened, we were sitting in the sun on the veranda, looking out over the garden, and my mother said, just like that, out of nowhere: *I hope we'll be able to take care of ourselves and won't be a burden on you, that we die on our own two feet and with our wits about us, that's what keeps us awake at night.*

You're just like that old woman, my father cut in, *who was*

always saying – no matter which of the two of us dies first, I'm
gonna go live with the kids.

I remember that afternoon and their words very clearly. And how nothing foreshadowed what was to come only three months later.

Without meaning to, you count every day after the end. You feel as if he just got up and stepped out of the living room to have a smoke on the balcony. Which, by the way, he did on the first few days when he came to Sofia.

As I open a little jar of home-made strawberry preserves, the thought of him pierces me. Only a few short months ago, this past summer, he and my mother had picked these strawberries. The dedication in the novel that brought them so much joy this year reads: '*To my mother and father, who are still weeding the eternal strawberry fields of childhood*'. Do I need to change the 'still'?

48

On one of the first days after his funeral, his phone suddenly rang. I was alone in the room and, naturally, was startled. His mobile was one of those older models, with a little screen. Only after the third ring did I pick up; I had planned just to let it ring, but then I decided to answer after all. *Hello . . . Dinyo, hope you're not sleeping . . .* (Every comment sounds absurd in this context and full of double meaning) . . . *Uhh*, I start to say, but the person on the other end is already on a roll. *What's going on, I heard you were under the weather, isn't it high time you got up out of bed already . . . It's not Dinyo*, I interrupt him, *it's his son . . . my father . . . passed away*. A brief silence. Rustling in the receiver at the other end, *But what do you mean, that's . . .* awkward condolences and then he hangs up. After death, the telephone is a source of metaphysical horror.

I tell my wife about this incident, and in response she tells me the following story, which she heard from one of her students. The student in question was working at a call centre for one of the national mobile operators. In the middle of the night, a woman rang and said through her sobs: *I got a call from such-and-such a number, it's my husband's, but we buried him a few days ago. Where is his phone now?* the young man asked. *Well, it's with him, we put it in the coffin, but I just got the call a little bit ago. Did you pick up? Well, not at first, I was scared, then I decided to call him back, but he didn't answer.*

Sometimes this happens, the young man said, trying to insert some common sense back into the conversation, *the battery simply runs out and some cells get activated . . . If you're concerned, you could call the cemetery or . . . the police.*

What the hell should be done in such instances? Is there some standard protocol to follow? And whom should we turn to – the police, the undertaker or the Gospel?

As if it's not enough to suffer the death of your loved one, do phones, cells and wires really have to get mixed up in it, too (you've got calls from this number)? Technology has clearly stormed into this forbidden territory as well.

For this reason, the aged Hans Christian Andersen, when he went to bed in the evening, always put a little note on his bedside table that read 'I'm not dead, only sleeping.' Just in case. I wonder, however, when he finally did die one day, whether they ignored the note or patiently waited a day or two just to make sure he wouldn't wake up?

I haven't erased my father's number from my phone. Not yet. I don't know if I ever will. I wondered whether to leave his watch with him. It's a different time zone there. Or there are no times and no zones. Then I remembered how often he looked at it at the end, in his final minutes. And I left it on his wrist.

49

It was December, the day of the funeral, and the garden, his pride and joy, looked deserted and unkempt. But as the son of a gardener, I knew this was merely an illusion. Two slender snowdrops had pushed up through the soil right next to the front door. *Will we wait for the snowdrops?* That had been one of his questions to the doctor. This year the snowdrops came too late.

I looked at the barren garden, which only a month or two later would be unrecognisable as the seeds buried there burst forth. I thought about *the force that through the green fuse drives the flower* . . . My father had put himself into the snowdrops, the hyacinth, the primrose (or cowslip, as he called it), the yellow of the daffodil, the red and white of the tulip, the magenta of the peony, and the raging white, yellow, red, purple and pink of the various sorts of roses. The air would be weighted with nameless scents, the bees would float about heavily, drunk on everything, in their buzzing Zen. My father, the gardener, would appear, invisible behind some bush, to mutter something under his breath, to smell the roses, to get rid of some unneeded branch. And only Jacko the dog would stop for a moment, staring straight ahead, then he would start barking and jumping, wagging his tail happily with a joy that would remain inexplicable to us.

My father did leave us some final words after all. I told myself, we'll read them in spring.

50

And then I discovered it – not that he had hidden it, but rather I opened it for the first time. My father's notebook. His only diary, kept in his final years. When I say *diary*, the word is misleading, you won't find anything personal inside, but that's how Bulgarian diaries are. More like notes from the field of everyday life, with a practical focus. (Which is how writing itself arose, incidentally – as far as we know, the first evidence of writing was a clay tablet upon which someone recorded the number of sheep or swine, I can't remember.)

There is no strong tradition of personal diaries, epistolary novels and the like in Bulgarian life, not in the past century, nor in the more distant past. This is part of our innate muteness about all things personal. It's always a well-kept secret, more closely guarded even than that barrel of wine in the cellar or brandy distilled behind closed doors to avoid the taxman.

But if you look, some strange tradition of notebooks or notes in the margins of other books can be found. My great-grandfather, my father's favourite grandfather, left behind just such a small notebook, where the bulk of the notes record how many olives or how much cheese he bought, how much money he spent and whom he sold what to, when the cow calved and so on – in short, notes about the economics of his tiny private enterprise. When private enterprise disappeared and the family's cows, horses and sheep were taken away, there was nothing left for my grandfather to write down. For this reason, he did not keep a notebook. To a certain extent, the notebook was now being kept by the leadership of the collective farm or by the Party itself.

Yet my grandfather still found a way to leave a written trace. In our old family Bible, which my grandmother hid in the wooden chest, slyly wrapped in the official socialist-era newspaper, *Worker's Deed*, on the blank pages in the back, he had written several lines with a chemical pencil. (A brief tangent – a chemical pencil was a more labour-intensive writing implement, you had to wet it or spit on it to write. This was the same pencil my grandfather taught me to write my first letters with, and our tongues were always purple like *karakondzhuli* ghouls from Bulgarian folklore.) Several lines, written in his own hand at the end of the Bible, right after the Apocalypse of St John, also known as the Book of Revelation, noted when *little Kalé* had passed away, the daughter they lost at the age of four, then when their next daughter was born and christened with the same name, when they married her off, the death of his father, and my father's wedding.

With this, the entirety of my grandfather's personal life was exhausted.

He could not be accused of wasting words. But I forgot – there in the first line, where he recorded the death of his daughter, he added two words, *milo chedo*, dear child, repeated twice right above it, and there the pencil was a deeper blue. For a person who was taught to swallow back the personal, those two words are a true revelation, grief worthy of Homer's muse.

51

So here it is, after that whole brief family epistles, my father's notebook. A small, black, hardback notebook, lined. Begun at the start of this final year, covered in his slanted, sweeping handwriting. We can safely dub this 'The Gardener's Diary'. He has made notes about every day that he worked in the garden, when he planted, when he sprayed, when he watered . . . He noted all this with a purely practical aim, I tell myself, so as not to forget and to keep track of when he needed to water again after several days, how long it had been since he last sprayed, when the soil was last turned over and so on. The diary itself begins in February simply because in January there is no gardening to be done.

17 February – planted 20 holes of fava beans. Also planted a kilo of onion sets and 1 packet of spinach and parsley.

18 February – pruned back the trees.

21 March – planted 8 kilos of potatoes.

The potatoes we would eat when he was no longer with us.

A month later, on 21 April, he put in fifty tomato plants. The tomatoes we would eat that same summer and autumn were enormous and actually tasted like tomatoes. The notes continue with the planting of zucchini and sweetcorn, as well as the first spraying against pests.

Now my brother uses this notebook as a gardening handbook for the things he wants to plant in the garden. And the notebook really helps with this. But I read it through the handwriting, and through what has been noted. I try to see my father behind these specific notes, I imagine him bent over the rows of tomatoes, for example, I imagine how afterwards he sits down on the veranda outside the house at sunset, lights up a cigarette (his first round of cancer did not put him off smoking), opening up the notebook and recording the day.

May has arrived. He has seven months left. He's sprayed the tomatoes, cucumbers and fruit trees. The date is 7 May, the day after St George's Day. *Planted the cannas and the dahlias* – flowers whose folk names he knew. *On 11 May – watered the potatoes, watered the cucumbers, watered the peppers, hoed the second half of the empty space.*

Days follow, full of watering, spraying, raking or hand-tilling, yet more hoeing, working on the rows of strawberries, the endless labour of May. There is only one day off – 28 May, *we went to a memorial for Zhoro, gone eight years now.* The first noting of something different in the notebook, a memorial for his best friend and cousin who was like a brother to him. And yet another different note in this jam-packed May. *Went to Sofia with D. for the showing of the film about G.* I remember how excited they were and how little time I managed to spend with them then.

The next day, the work in the garden continues at full steam, the pages of the notebook are crammed with writing. *Hoed . . . harvested . . . cleaned . . . watered . . .* The whole whirlwind of early June. There isn't a single empty day. Except for 26 June – *it rained.* There's half a year left until the end. Surely he must have been in pain already.

You know, I get tired out real quick, he tells me. *Well, you're doing the work of a whole summer brigade,* I reply. In July the tasks in the garden continue the same as before – *watering, spraying, harvesting, cleaning up the grasses, hoeing . . .* In August, the work changes slightly – *picked tomatoes, we made 30 jars of salsa, picked peppers, then roasted them on sheet metal and in the chushkopek, weeded the strawberries . . . 27 August – we went to the graveyard.*

It's strange, that second note about going to the graveyard, amid the peppers, tomatoes and watering, it's as if it wasn't meant for this notebook.

And so the autumn starts. In September, only several short, repeating phrases: *9 September – roasted peppers.* This makes me laugh – he did not fail to fire up the pepper roaster on that erstwhile socialist holiday, even though the mandatory demonstrations have long since disappeared. *10 September – watered the greenhouse. 14 September – watered the greenhouse . . .*

The 16th of September is his birthday, but there's nothing in the notebook. I had called him that day, and he had said that in the evening he'd decided to take my brother's family out to a nice restaurant in town. He had just got his pension and a little money from the village fields he rented out. I asked him how he was. *I'm fine*, he said, *something's a little tight in my lower back, but it's because I was hauling some scraps of metal around the garden . . .*

I need to take something out of that first-aid kit of first-rate stories, and then we'll go on.

52

First-rate, first-aid stories.

The one about that local guy who was staggering home drunk from the neighbouring village, but passed out in the cemetery and fell asleep on top of a random grave. It was All Souls' Day, so in the morning the village women started cackling at him – *What the dickens are you doin' here, you ain't one of our boys!* So our man shook himself awake, got up off the grave he'd blacked out on, looked at the unfamiliar stone cross, and uttered the phrase that made the story infamous and worth retelling: *Ah well, here I was wondering why I'm a wreck even though I'm not that sad – I've got the wrong graveyard!*

Or the one about that old man in the fifties who was caught selling potatoes on the black market to make some extra cash and was taken down to the People's Militia for a beating. So he said – *Well now, since you're gonna beat me over the potatoes anyway, go ahead and beat me for the red pepper I sold this summer so we can get it over with in one go.* We would all howl with laughter, while my father lit up a cigarette and repeated – *so we can get it over with in one go . . .*

Or the one about the traffic cop from the next village over, who was so honest that when he himself committed even the tiniest infraction – say he crossed the divider line or drove five kilometres over the speed limit – would stop his motorcycle, get off, salute, scold himself and write himself a ticket.

I suspect he'd heard some of these stories elsewhere, but just as he grafted the branches of fruit trees onto wild saplings, he also skilfully grafted these tales onto local people and places, and they would blossom and bear fruit when he told them.

53

The last note in my father's black notebook for September is from the 25th.

And it says: *Wat. grhs.* He had gathered the strength to water the greenhouse, but not to finish his note. Like a graphologist who has arrived too late, I try to decipher the level of pain that makes you abbreviate both words like that. There were no abbreviations in his previous notes. The date on the next page is much further on: 28 October 2023, he's written the year as well for the first time.

He hasn't written anything for more than a month between 25 September and 28 October. This lacuna is the most painful one in the notebook. A month of silence. Clearly he was starting to experience a lot of pain, his body began giving out, or he no longer saw the point in keeping notes.

The handwriting in the final note is slightly different, in large, almost printed letters that go outside the lines he has written:

DICLOPRAM FOR PAIN

He has underlined it twice.

For the first and last time, the word *pain* appears here. He has less than two months left. In the context of the mutcness, with which his generation – and the generations of men before him – treated the expression of personal feelings, those three words are the equivalent of a howl, a wail. You might not even hear it at all, not realise the intensity of the pain, just as those of us around him did not. Even the word *pain* here is mentioned in relation to the medication, not within a personal confession.

I remember that on 8 October, on one of those days without an entry in the notebook, I was there, in the garden. In the evening, he, my mother, and I went to the theatre in town to watch a play based on a selection of my stories, entitled *All Our Bodies*. An elderly actor in the troupe was playing him, my father, even using his name. In the last scene, he lies dying in the hospital, surrounded by all his bodies at different ages. One by one, they took their leave of him and filed out. The last one remaining was the boy he had been when he was young. The boy took him by the hand and led him to the door. *It's good for someone to see you to the door . . .*

What was he thinking as he watched that scene? I wonder now. We talked a bit afterwards, I don't think they liked the play much. But he stayed for a glass of wine, he laughed, talked to everyone. All the actors were looking at him with deep respect, as if he had just stepped out of the play itself. He didn't say he was in pain, he was full of energy, he was having a good time, or so it seemed to me. We got back to the village house late that night. I slept there and left the next day, calmer. Just as I was leaving, I recall that I said (under the purple rose bush), with all the gravity I could muster, that he should stop working on the garden, otherwise he might suddenly collapse. I took off for Lisbon. We decided that when I got back, we'd go to the doctor to see about that pain in his lower back. He agreed and said that he'd come to Sofia for a day or two so they could give him a shot of something and then he'd come back to the village. As I left, we hugged for longer than usual. He could tell I was worried, and so he told me: *There's nothing to fear, I'll wait . . .*

54

I ponder the fact that the last time I was here, in the village house, and he was alive, was just two or so months ago. The last roses of October were blooming then. The dahlias along the fence were stretching up high, my father pointing at them with pride; two months later some of them would be lying on his grave. Now I'm walking through the December yard, noticing how the first signs of desolation are starting to show. Needles from the pine tree are scattered around the veranda, some old leaves are rotting in the corner (he would never have allowed this). It's not just people who cannot live without houses, houses cannot live without their people, either.

Gardening and death. It seems to me that gardening is fundamentally in opposition to death. In the garden, you are always burying something and then waiting for a miracle to occur, for it to sprout, to become something different from the seed you sowed, green and slender, with leaves and flowers, with fruit, something different, yet also a repetition, the same thing, *flesh of its flesh* (language thinks primarily in metaphors from the animal kingdom). The idea of resurrection is, I think, a botanical idea. This is where the allegory came from, that's what started it. Immortality is also a botanical idea. All plants, which we view as less evolved than us, actually know one more miracle than we do, they have one more superpower. They know how to die in such a way that they can come back to life again.

What happens to the garden in front of the house, when the gardener is gone? The cherries will ripen and fall, the apples will ripen and fall, the pears, the plums . . . The grass will begin to overtake the path. The garden will continue to flourish, even without its gardener, what he has planted will still grow, bear fruit, but wildness will also start to make inroads, after some time weeds and grasses will overtake everything. Perhaps not immediately, but eventually that is the way of things – bodies go cold, gardens go wild, children are orphaned. And yet in a certain sense, though the gardener is mortal, the garden is immortal. Perhaps it will no longer be a garden exactly. The creation of a garden involves complex manoeuvres, wars and truces with nature, sometimes you are on her side, you use what has been seeded, soil and fertility, yet at the same time you wage a battle to control and cultivate her. These weeds – let's get rid of them; these bushes – they can stay; the roses – fine, but with brutal pruning.

In fact, five months later I see just this. The single surviving red rose has muscled its way up, its fantastic blossoms tower at over two metres, taller than I am, I can't even sniff them. We are used to bending over a rose to smell it. Bending over, we offer a subconscious obeisance to the gardener who has tended the rose, but also to the gardener who has tended the idea of the rose.

What happened to the Garden of Eden after it was abandoned? Did it go to seed?

55

While I'm writing this book, April is nearing its end. This is the precise moment when the yellow dandelions turn to white puffs. Here, where I'm writing, in my hiding place, the dandelion puffs are enormous. From time to time, the breeze carries away a bit of fluff. But they know that this is part of the game of life, not of death.

The nearby meadows are sprinkled with bluebells and daisies. Here and there I discover forget-me-nots. The clouds in April are light and watercoloured, rolling and scattered like dandelion fluff. Cows are grazing somewhere nearby, I first catch the scent, then I hear the bells. A train with two carriages cuts through the valley with a funny *fyuuuu* sound, as if from another time.

My brother sends me photos of my father's garden. The peonies are going crazy, as he would say, the daffodils gleam along the netted fence. My favourite light-purple rose bush has started to bloom, I can smell it even from here, where I'm writing, two thousand kilometres away from the garden. Jacko the dog is prancing about, waiting for my father to show up. I think someone should tell the roses, too, that my father is gone, so they're not left wondering.

Death, explained for roses and dogs. Of course, we know about death and dying, the roses would reply with a huff; after all, we do it every winter.

56

A month after his death, my daughter is the only one of us who dreams about him often. *Last night I dreamed about grandpa as a kid, he looked happy.* The day after that, she tells me her latest dream. She and her friends are playing in the garden in front of the house. They've all climbed up into the trees and are waiting for the cats to come. Allow me to go on a brief tangent here. When she was little, my father looked after fourteen cats in the yard. Like every child, she loved cats and dogs; I think that's why my father collected them, though it horrified my mother. *You need to come up with names for them all*, he told her once, *because I can't tell them apart any more.* So she got to work. She took each of them into her lap, petted it, looked it over carefully for some identifying feature, and gave out names. *This one is Stripey (can't you see the stripe here on his head), this one is Foxy, you're Bunny 'cause of your big ears, these two'll be the Pharaohs* (a chunky pair of twins) and so on.

Anyway, so now in her dream she and her friends are waiting for that whole feline host to fill the garden. *We were a little scared*, she says. Then she realises that she hasn't got the food ready. She climbs down from the tree, goes over to the dish and . . . this was clearly the scariest part of the dream, *the bowl was totally mouldy, unwashed, neglected for months, and I really got scared*, she said.

Your grandpa didn't appear in that dream? I asked.

She looked at me, puzzled.

I told you, the cats' dish had been left mouldy and neglected.

Of course, death can look like that, too.

57

At the end of January, we gather at the far end of the cemetery, at the highest point, where my father lies. It's the first major memorial day according to local custom, forty days after death. It is cold and windy. To our left are the last apartment blocks on the outskirts of the town, right in front of him stretch the endless lowland fields, now just dirt and mud. Elderly relatives, my father's generation, some from the villages around the town, each with their own flower, lean on their walking sticks, limping and crooked; they huddle together for warmth, like veterans of an invisible war they don't recall waging. My brother sets up a folding table, on which he places a large ritual bowl of boiled wheat. The wheat is still warm, and steam rises from it in the frosty January air. He pours a little into a cup for each person. As he hands me mine, he whispers in my ear: *If you want to dream about him, you have to eat the wheat here, at his grave.* I've told him that I've hardly dreamed about our father since his passing. The wind is so strong that it blows all the candles out. I look around and see that the plots around my father have filled up; only forty days ago his grave was the only one here.

My father's new neighbours. I look at the photos on their

headstones, ordinary people from the town and villages, some of whom he may have passed by in the street. Then I suddenly come across a name from China or Vietnam. In the 1980s, Vietnamese workers became part of the history of this town and others around Bulgaria. We bought our first digital watches from them on the black market. And my first cassette player too. Just like that, smuggled via Vietnam, a sliver of the outside world slipped in.

I am sure that my father immediately started chatting to his neighbours, that he already knows everything about them and tells them stories in the evenings.

Strangely enough, now I dream of him most often when I'm abroad, when I travel far away. The dreams always begin as calm as can be: nothing out of the ordinary, my father is alive, he's in the garden, I walk over to him. And it's only when I go to hug him that the doubt strikes me that perhaps he isn't alive. And I wonder whether my hands will meet his body or whether they'll pass right through him like a hologram. I wake up immediately.

My daughter reports something similar. *I dreamed that he was alive, but I know that shouldn't be the case, so I tell him flat out: How on earth can you be here, you've got a death certificate after all. And he says – They've made a mistake and let me out for a month. And we're pretending to be happy,* my daughter says, *but actually we're afraid, because we know he'll be in pain again.*

58

In a culture where it is not customary to say things like *I love you, I feel so bad for you, I miss you*, and so on, people find different ways to express their love. I have already written elsewhere that our mother cooked up fantastic *banitsi* out of her silence. Just as my father took care of the garden. And what a garden it was! I suspect these were their declarations of love for us. But my brother and I would say – *Give it a rest already, why are you ruining your health with all that hoeing, watering and weeding, only for either drought or worms to destroy half of it in the end? We could buy all this from the shop just as easily.*

We said this, of course, because we could see he was exhausted. I now know that he was producing something else. Something that cannot be found at the shop.

One day he told me – *Those razors you brought back for me from Germany, they're quite the thing, they've lasted me a whole year.* That was an expression of feeling, too. *I'll get some more for you, I'll be travelling there again soon. No need to go overboard*, he said, *there'll be enough. We're not gonna live forever like the eagles, after all.* Yet another one of his favourite phrases.

I bought him seven razors. And while I was buying them, his words ran through my head. I wondered whether, if I bought ten or fifty or a hundred, I could lengthen his days. Because how could you die when you had so many nice, brand-new German razors?

59

I had the tallest father of my childhood. Damn, how proud I was of that! I've saved two photos, small black and white prints, with the zigzagged edges typical of that time. And in both of them, my father is holding me in his arms. In the first, I'm a few months old. He himself, also a newborn father, holds me rather awkwardly; clearly he has been given strict instructions – one arm here, support the neck with the other arm so the baby's head won't flop back. (I, too, many years later, held my daughter in that same awkward way.) He was twenty-four then, while I was thirty-nine when my daughter was born. In the photo his head touches the trellis he stands under, the vine leaves curling around his forehead like a true Dionysus. In his arms, I, too, am exactly that tall for a moment.

The other photo was taken about two years later. I'm much bigger now, and he is holding me much more confidently. Two metres high again, I am looking at the world from above with a slight frown, but I'm not afraid. We will never be as safe as we once were in our father's arms.

Childhood is vertical. You grow upwards, you're as tall as the roses in the garden, everyone tells you year after year how much you've grown, your father lifts you up high, you get up on your tiptoes, everything buzzes with life and motion, you don't want to go to bed, they can only make you by force. Old age is horizontal. Let's rest a bit, lie down after lunch, just let me stretch out here on the couch, 'cause my back . . . Old age is getting used to a long, perhaps eternal, horizontality.

When I think about him, I see him simultaneously at all his different ages, even as a child. In all the bodies of those different ages. From this point of view, you can grasp everything and everyone. This is perhaps the point of view that Augustine, Boethius, and others after them wrote about. Outside of linear time, there, where the one looking down on us from above sees all at once our past, present and future.

60

The absent father from communist times. Isn't absence actually an essential part of the father's character in literature all over the world? Fathers are serving at the front or in prison, or looking for the golden fleece, or lounging with nymphs on distant islands, or getting caught in a storm on their way home, or hanging out in the dive bars of the world, or they're off somewhere working abroad, making money, or they simply don't feel like coming home . . .

In Christianity, the iconic image is, of course, the Madonna and Child. You rarely see the earthly father Joseph with the baby Jesus in his arms. The Father and Child is practically nonexistent. There are a few exceptions, but these very exceptions seem to hint at how awkward this whole situation is and how there's no way it'll enter the canon. Take, for example, Guido Reni's seventeenth-century painting, *St Joseph with the Infant Jesus*. We see the white-haired, white-bearded Joseph holding in his aged hands (a carpenter's hands) the chubby baby Jesus, who is active and lively, somehow even restless, reaching out with his right hand to play with the old man's beard.

The righteous Joseph appears so infrequently in the four

Gospels that he could easily be overlooked, unlike the omnipresent Mary. In Matthew, we see him mostly as an errand boy, following the orders of the angel who appears in his dreams – *Accept this woman, don't abandon her, take the child and go here and there.* The Gospel pays little attention to what Joseph is going through, how he comes to terms with the idea of the *enceinte* Virgin Mary. Thankfully, the Troparions and liturgical texts offer us more insight into Joseph's internal anguish about accepting the miracle of the Immaculate Conception. In Luke, however, references to Joseph are even scarcer. And in a majority of paintings, his presence is on a par with that of the ox and the ass around the manger, as he stands somewhere in the back, looking pensive.

Later, when Jesus is around twelve, his father disappears completely, most likely he dies (but not before teaching his son the craft of carpentry, though this does not turn out to be of much use to him). Joseph does not witness his son's breathtaking trajectory, he will not feel pride at seeing the disciples who follow him, he will be gone before the most crucial moment, the Crucifixion, he will not mourn his son's death, nor will the latter appear to him in a dream to announce his Resurrection, apart from in a few apocryphal stories in which this occurs, but the Apocrypha are always more merciful than the canonical texts. There's no room for two fathers in the canon. And the righteous Joseph has made his peace with that.

The father only shows up when the baby is already two years old, a friend of mine liked to joke. We, the children of socialism, grew up without fathers in a certain sense. If socialism, in its rather wooden way, claimed that 'the family is the smallest unit of society', then surely the father was not the most reliable part of that unit. Fathers drank, played cards and told jokes. Plus, it wasn't at all clear what their backgrounds were, whether they were caught up in the Militia's disciplinary measures or whether they listened to forbidden radio stations in the kitchen at night. Incidentally, my father fits this character type almost to a T.

Children were supposed to grow up nurtured by the Party and its youth subdivisions – school and the Chavdar/Pioneer/Komsomol organisation, that three-headed dragon of ideology and pedagogy. Your day should be filled with various clubs and activities – clubs for the young aeronautical engineer, the young biologist, the young builder – or with gathering recyclables, picking chamomile or working on the autumn harvest brigades to support the collective farms, so as not to have spare time to think about jeans, Black Sabbath or other such nonsense. Parents were at work all day in any case, so they didn't have anything against someone keeping us busy.

61

Again, sometime back in childhood, one of my basic fears was that I was adopted. I have no idea why, but I've come to realise that this was a fairly widespread fear across our entire generation. Perhaps because such things were considered a dirty secret at the time, and everyone had heard those awful whispers: did you know that he's adopted, or that girl's adopted, can you imagine, hoo-wee . . .

Proof seemed to come to me uninvited. I don't have any photos of myself at the maternity ward as a baby, which confirms that I'm not their child. Most likely those photos are still with my true parents. But there's something else that keeps me awake at night. My mother and father have dark-brown eyes, yet mine are light, bluish-green. OK fine, so my brother has blue-green eyes as well. That means they adopted both of us.

Sometimes, to test my suspicions, I would ask them very casually – *What do you remember about when I was born?* I noticed that they didn't pay much attention to my questions, which could only mean they were avoiding answering. I became even more duplicitous in my investigations (I had secretly leafed through my mother's criminology textbook, she's a lawyer). I would lie in wait to question them separately, to compare their testimony. I must admit their stories coincided, but nevertheless this did not dispel my doubts, because, of course, all criminals agree upon an alibi. (Hang on a second now, what's this talk of 'criminals'? Even if I had been adopted, it wouldn't be a crime.) Anyway, their memories were of a major snowstorm, a Jeep covered with a canvas tarp flying from the village towards the maternity ward in the town of Y, a difficult birth, cold rooms heated with coal, haemorrhaging, being saved, a large baby, and so on. I'm not sure how long my doubts would have lasted if I hadn't found salvation in a college biology textbook I happened upon. There it said that parents with brown eyes can have children with blue eyes, especially if the parents' parents have that genetic trait. And it explained all this with a simple table of Xs and Ys. Now I know this is the theory of recessive genes, but then it literally re-established my mother and father's parenthood.

62

So it seems that it is not just in Christianity and socialism that the father is an absent figure. Isn't absence in fact the fundamental, defining characteristic of the father in the long-ago myth of Odysseus, for example? And isn't Odysseus himself a towering figure in culture, the archetype of this absence? We are mesmerised by his story, full of obstacles and adventures. But how would it sound if told by his son, Telemachus? A kind of mournful cry for his father, but presumably not without reproach: you were gone just when I needed you most, when the other kids bragged about their fathers and used them as a threat – I'll tell my dad, I swear; you weren't there to help with my first shave; you weren't there to teach me how to fight. You weren't there . . .

Odysseus the father appears only when his son is twenty and has already come of age – not dissimilar to the experience of my generation with the missing fathers of socialism. Yet I doubt Telemachus ever loved anyone more than his father. The way we love those who are absent. Indeed, Telemachus is the only person whose loyalty Odysseus does not test.

And yet another scene that has been left in the shadows.

At the end, after his return to Ithaca, after meeting the loyal swineherd, after seeing his son Telemachus and the faithful Penelope, only in the twenty-fourth and very last song does Odysseus go to see his own elderly father (the fathers are always saved for the very end). He finds him doing what? Working his garden of all things, an orchard, digging up a vine, then turning his attention to a sapling. Upon seeing Laertes crushed by old age and grief, Odysseus hides behind a leafy tree and bursts into tears. Then he decides to approach the old man, without giving himself away, and starts up a conversation about his garden.

Old man, you know your trade and take good care of this neat garden. Every plant and vine, and tree – the figs, the pears, the olive trees – and bed of herbs is nicely tended.

All of this, only to tell him immediately afterwards: *You do not take good care of your own self.* Clearly something that all sons tell their fathers.

Odysseus reveals himself to his father, but must give proof that it is really him, the son of Laertes. So he offers two pieces of evidence – the first is a scar from a boar's tooth, while the second relates to the garden. He recalls a memory of running at his father's heels as a young boy in that very garden: *When I was little, I would follow you around the garden, asking all their names. We walked beneath these trees; you named them all and promised them to me.* This is followed by a catalogue, not of ships like in *The Iliad*, but of fruit trees.

Ten apple trees, and thirteen pear trees, forty figs, and fifty grapevines which ripen one by one . . .

Such is the father's perpetual gift: fruit trees and vines. And this gift is never-ending, because it renews itself every year.

My father recreated Laertes's gift without knowing it.

As I read these verses, an ancient sorrow and humility, or rather Homerility, fills me. It's so beautiful that I leave off writing and go outside. I feel the need to gaze at the sky, and of course, it too is somehow Homeric, as ancient Greek clouds drift in the evening hour.

63

It is harder to write about fathers. Perhaps this is because an invisible umbilical cord to the mother remains intact throughout our childhoods: she is somewhere near you, she makes your lunch, she takes care of you when you're sick, puts her hand on your forehead, she is the air you swim in. The father is a different sort of presence – shadowy, mysterious, sometimes frightening, often absent, clinging to the snorkel of a cigarette, he swims in other waters and clouds.

All the literature in the world – Bulgarian is no exception – praises the mother and writes bitter, Kafkaesque letters to the father.

Once, in response to a question about where his father worked, one of my classmates replied – *At the slap factory.* For a few seconds, the teacher mechanically accepted this as correct information and started writing it down in the register. All fathers at that time worked in some sort of factory – for porcelain, rubber or bricks, so why not at a slap factory as well? Then she realised what was going on and shot all of us a stern look, while we died of laughter.

Yet the slap factory not only existed, it worked full steam, churning out slaps on a conveyor belt. *Don't make me turn on the slap factory* – we heard this warning regularly if we even dared think about doing something forbidden. Usually our fathers worked there, they themselves were the slap factories, but our mothers were not above it either. Nor were our teachers. And this whole industry started well before our time. They say that in the 1884 Rule Book of the Gabrovo School, one of the first in Bulgaria, it says: 'The school accepts only children who are grown up and can take a beating.'

Slapping someone's cheek or pulling their ear was absolutely in the normal swing of things. *I'll box your ears* was no metaphor or hyperbole; my brother's form teacher really did slightly tear the lower part of his ear lobe, as the school doctor confirmed. I have memories of chalk being thrown at me and being hit by the pointer, but it was the raps to the head from the German teacher that were the most painful, thanks to the metal ring she wore. (I used to wonder whether German teachers were crueller than French teachers, or whether the language had nothing to do with it.)

Nevertheless, the most terrifying threat from that time was always, *I'm going to tell your father!* The father had to be the bogeyman, the disciplinarian. And in most cases, he was. *Where is Kiril? His folks are looking for him to give him a good beating* – this remained one of the most popular lines from Bulgarian children's films. Some of my classmates even bragged about what a thrashing they'd got or what hidings awaited them that evening.

For better or for worse, our father didn't have to actually

beat us. He was so tall and gruff that he only had to squint his eyes and purse his lips, which he did very expressively, and we wouldn't dare move a muscle. One of the most common punishments back then was being locked up in a dark cellar for a period of time. Making you a Minotaur for an hour or two. I have a vague memory of this happening to me and my brother once. And even though my father couldn't stand it and let us out after only ten or fifteen minutes, it felt like we had spent an entire eternity among ghosts, rats and canning jars. In the dark, time passes in a different way.

Much later, sometime in 2016, I rewatched all the classic Bulgarian children's movies I could find. Afterwards I 'sliced out' of them every scene with slaps, ear-pulling, headlocks, smacks upside the head . . . I edited all the scenes together and got two and half minutes of good thrashing, as it was called back then. I entitled it 'The Slap Factory'. My daughter, who was then nine, heard the phrase and asked – *Daddy, what's a slap?*

I had no idea there was so much smacking going on in cinema. Some of the scenes were quite realistic. The video played for two weeks, projected on a gallery wall, and at the end of the fortnight I gathered visitors together to recount the first time they had been slapped. Or the slap they will never forget. As soon as they started speaking, many people's voices broke and they couldn't go on. There were others who turned the story into a joke, saying that's how it was back then and that actually, they'd deserved it.

And do you remember the first time you slapped someone? I had asked. I'll never forget those five long minutes of silence before somebody spoke up.

64

Well now, I'll just toast myself a piece of fatback bacon on the coals, I'll cut off a hunk of bread and drink some red wine . . . Something else my father said, he who could barely swallow a slice of tangerine. *Just say the word, I would tell him* – and I was ready to find both the fatback and the coals. *If only I could*, my father would reply. *Pour me a sip of red wine. If the horse dies, let it be from too much grain!* Another one of his favourite sayings. He pressed the cup to his lips, just enough to wet them, without taking a sip, and then set it aside.

A sudden wave of sorrow as I boil an egg for breakfast.

A lump in my throat simply because on a sunny winter afternoon, the snow was piled high and he would have said – I can hear his voice now – how good that would be for the garden. I take my mother out for a walk, we stroll slowly because she tires easily, her haemoglobin is critically low, we sit down on a bench and let the sun pass through us. Without speaking.

Since my father passed away, a strange silence has fallen.

65

There is a painting by Edvard Munch – *Death and the Child* from 1889. I came across it years ago in a museum in Bremen. A blondish five- or six-year-old child stands with its face turned towards us and its back to the bed, where its dying (or already dead) mother lies. Munch himself was five when his mother passed away. The child's blue, wide-open eyes gaze out with fear and despair. But what made me stand for so long before that painting was another detail: the child is shown pressing its hands tightly over its ears. I don't want to hear anything, don't tell me! (The whole figure is reminiscent of *The Scream*, the famous painting that would be exhibited for the first time four years later. For now, the scream is only in the body, it is building up, but has no escape hatch yet; the horror is quiet.)

It's as if what is heard can be more terrifying that what is seen. Only words can seal a death certificate. As long as no one says she's dead, he's dead, there's still hope.

Years later, my daughter – who was then, at five or six, the same age as Munch's child – and I found ourselves in the hallway of a provincial hospital, where her other grandfather had fallen into a coma. I will never forget that derelict emergency room with its half-broken fluorescent lights, one of them dangling precipitously, flickering on and off constantly, turning the hallway itself into an ambulance of sorts. And what did the child do? She stood with her back to all of us at the end of the corridor and covered her ears with her hands, not knowing that she was stepping into a Munch painting.

66

While my father was dying, I often tried to bring him back to his childhood. Back to those territories where you are immortal, pain has not yet arrived, and between you and death lie years which you are only now starting to cross. A naive attempt, because that generation did not have a childhood.

Amid all the family photos, there is only one of my father as a child. He's three or four, sitting in his mother's lap. They've dressed him up in a borrowed sailor suit. That's how he started out and until the very end he wore our hand-me-downs – clothes borrowed from me and my brother.

We know that childhood as a separate, protected period of life did not appear until quite late in human history, sometime during the sixteenth or seventeenth centuries in Europe, with the introduction of school. Yet even in the mid-twentieth century it continued to be threatened, especially in our part of the world. And especially for that generation born at the end of the war. The child was simply a small, not-yet fully grown adult. It wore hand-me-downs from bigger folks, and it waited in the wings until it turned six or seven and could join the family labour force.

I try to envisage my father at six, grazing the oxen in the meadow, a flask of water at his waist. He follows them through the grass, a thorn pierces his heel, he stops, pulls it out, catches up with the oxen, then something rustles nearby. I just hope it's not a viper; grass snakes, he knows, are not dangerous.

Then I imagine him at nine, woken by his father at three in the morning; it's cold and dark, he can barely shake off sleep, he hitches up the cart to drive the women out to the field to pick tobacco.

I want to sleep, my soul is asleep, but your grandpa keeps telling me – c'mon, you just gotta drive 'em out there, you'll pick a basket of tobacco before dawn and then you're free . . .

Free in this case means he'll grab his notebooks and go to school, where he'll doze at his desk, awakened by the teacher's pointer on his shaved head. In the open air of the evening he could go to watch a film projected on the wall of the school. *I dreamed those films more than I watched them*, he liked to say, *I would be falling asleep even during the opening credits.*

In middle school he had the chance to go on a trip abroad. When he told his mother, she found an unexpected way to veto this: *Wait just a little bit longer*, she said, *you'll have to do your army service and then you'll travel, your father traipsed halfway around the world as a soldier.* Halfway around the world in this case meant Serbia and Hungary in between the battles and ruins of the Second World War. In the absence of another war, my grandfather never received an invitation to travel again. My father, thank goodness, was not sent anywhere abroad during his mandatory military service.

67

Next, he went to a technical college in the nearby town. And even though the town was small and provincial, this changed things considerably. But the poverty remained the same. I see him clearly, just as he is in his stories – tall and thin, with his school uniform jacket and trousers two sizes too big (so he can wear them for longer). He and his schoolmates went to the vineyard in the late autumn after the harvest, wandering through the rows looking for some fallen grape or forgotten bunch. *It was just us and the crows*, he liked to say. In the late winter of the 1950s they would stroll along the Teary River in town (what a lovely name!) to gather up driftwood and stumps so they could dry them out and warm themselves beside those eternal 'Gypsy love' stoves in their dorm rooms. They would also go to the train station to scavenge briquettes left behind by the freight trains.

Once, the visor of his cap broke, he didn't have any money for a new one, but he couldn't show up at school without a cap. So he cut the cover of his chemistry book into a crescent, slathered it in black shoe polish and that did the trick. Several days later, however, he left it in the cafeteria.

It was found by none other than the chemistry teacher, who saw the cover peeking out from beneath the polish and was furious. He lined them all up and shouted: *'Now let's see who dares make a mockery of chemistry!'* Only my father stood there at attention, bare-headed, with no cap. *So my friends and I went to catch worms as fishing bait for that teacher*, he would finish off the story, *so we could at least scrape by with a D, we collected so many darn worms . . .*

But just then, when he was still in college in Radnevo, a miracle occurred: the Harlem Globetrotters film arrived in Bulgaria. The film was to be shown in a larger city nearby. For those village boys, this must have been an absolutely exceptional event. Not only were they showing an American film, but it was about living legends. The boys borrowed bikes from their wealthier classmates, pedalled thirty kilometres to Stara Zagora, and managed with their very last pennies to get in and watch it, standing room only. This is probably where my father's dreams of playing basketball were born. He was tall, he had all the requisite characteristics. He must've started practising in the college years that followed, and continued in the army as well . . . He travelled with the army team, he, who had never gone anywhere until then (in this way my grandma turned out to be right to a certain extent). His travels were all within Bulgaria, of course, but that's still part of the world. He was healthy and full of promise, he had good technique, the coach liked him and a bright future gleamed in front of him . . .

I imagine him going back to the village after his army service, a directionless, twenty-year-old kid. The coach sent a telegram inviting him to join the team in the regional capital, they'd give him bed and board to begin with. My father didn't know how to tell his parents; the truth was that he didn't even have the five quid in his pocket for a ticket to the city. One day he got up his courage to ask them, and they, being folks who had never left the village, presumably said – *What do you think you're doing, going to chase that ball around instead of getting a real job, plus you better be closer, so you can help out, no one's ever made good in the city* . . . And they refused to let him go. My father dithered for a few more days, not knowing what to do, he'd never gone against anything his mother and father said, so in the end he stayed. He was offered a job in the village, he met my mother, who was eighteen, he promised her father that she'd study in Sofia if she was accepted to the university there, they accepted her, she left, but he stayed back in the village. He went to Sofia a few times, he even once went to a match of the team that had wanted him to join, but he was too ashamed to talk to the coach, then I was born, then he tore the ligaments in his knee, and his other possible life tucked its tail between its legs and was never seen again.

68

I look at pictures of him with his friends from the sixties. Handsome twenty-year-old young men, all looking as if they had just stepped out of a black-and-white French film, their hair slicked back with a little pork lard. Tight trousers, on the very edge of legal, the kind of trousers the ever-watchful People's Militiamen sliced up with scissors. Like in that forbidden little ditty, *drainpipe trousers nice and tight, lemony trench coat fits just right*, which he himself loved to sing. Or another tune that ended just like this: *By Jeep the cops and their champs drive me to the labour camp.*

They didn't take him in a Jeep to the labour camp, but they did cut up his trousers once, while another time – even I remember this – they called him down to the local Party office and ordered him to cut his hair, get rid of his moustache (the whole moustache business really infuriated them, who knows why), and to cut me and my brother's hair, too, as we were starting to look like the Beatles. My father argued that we looked like the famous footballers Cruyff and Beckenbauer, but that didn't fly at the local Party headquarters. Before taking us down to the village barber, he called over his cousin, the village photographer, so he could immortalise us with our long hair; my brother was four, I was six. He also got his picture taken with his moustache and sideburns. We did not take photos of our shaved heads. My mother burst into sobs when she saw us, as if we'd been arrested, while my grandma said, *It's no big deal, now their hair'll grow back even thicker.*

Funny stories from his youth, which my father had such a knack for telling . . . This is where my soft spot for the sixties comes from, their nostalgia has become my own. Nostalgia for a time that never happened to me.

At the end of the sixties, when my mother was at the university in Sofia, my father would go to see her, but they would stay at a hotel even though they were already married because her landlady did not allow men in the house. There is one photo of them in the restaurant in Hotel Sofia, likely taken at my mother's graduation. Both of them are impossibly young, just past twenty, with innocent faces (I suspect that black-and-white photography makes faces more beautiful and innocent). My mother's classmates are all around them, most of whom went on to be famous lawyers and prosecutors. My father has a story about that evening as well. The story centres around how he was not able to figure out the revolving door of the Hotel Sofia. A group of my mother's classmates had taken her inside, while he was left alone outside. *I'm pushing on the door to open it, but no dice. I step back and see that it spins around for other people no problem. Surely it knows who's from Sofia and who's really a student. So I bide my time, waiting for my chance when nobody's around, I push it and it freezes up again. In the end your mother comes out to get me, I could've died of shame. How was I supposed to know that you shouldn't push those doors or they block up?*

After death, did he revisit all his bodies, I wonder, and which one did he stay inside the longest?

69

My father made great stories out of his little failures. And he sure did know how to fail.

In 1989, he was forty-five, now I'd say *only* forty-five. The fall of the Wall and the entrance into the meat-grinder of the nineties jerked several generations out of their former lives. My parents' generation had it the worst, perhaps. They lost their jobs, factories and industries collapsed, owners changed, the more clued-in folks brashly took out loans they never paid back.

Along with many others, my father was left unemployed, so he decided to take the high road and try his hand at business. He failed at every attempt, of course. The previous year, there had been a terrible deficit of onions. As one acquaintance used to say back in socialist times – *When there's onions, there's only onions everywhere, and when there's no onions, there's none anywhere.*

So, my father decided that, according to all the laws of the new free market, since there was a deficit and a certain thing was being sought after, then it simply must be produced. He borrowed some money, we rented a few acres of land, planted onions, hoed it like crazy and got a bumper crop. Then we rounded up all our relatives; I had just got married, so we called in all my wife's relatives as well, and over several days of hard labour we dug up all the onions and lined them up in sacks. We built a new Berlin Wall of onions.

Everything was going according to my father's plan, and now we just needed to find a market. And here's where things went south. He set out to find buyers for his onions. First, he went around to the neighbouring villages – they didn't want any, they had plenty of their own, then he tried the whole district – nobody wanted onions. He headed across the country, reaching even the most far-flung little towns – but no and no again. This year, everybody had planted onions because of the deficit. He came back, crushed. He sat down in front of our wall of onions, which was taller than he was, and gloomily smoked a cigarette while my mother gazed on sternly. The worst part was that the onions started to rot, creating a deathly stench. We gave away as many as we could to relatives. And then my father set off to figure out where he could dump the rest. I think the whole of Bulgaria reeked of rotting onions that autumn.

Similar unsuccessful attempts, let's not call them failures, also occurred when he tried to raise ducks, to cultivate silkworms, to keep beehives and harvest honey, to start a small pig farm, a small agricultural collective, to revive an old mill . . . My father was looking more and more like the Don Quixote of agrarian entrepreneurship. The resemblance was physical too – tall, thin and ever more stooped, like a charcoal drawing by Picasso . . . He supposedly did everything right, but nothing ever worked out in the end. And this was more likely a sign of those rather shady times, than any ineptitude on his part.

70

Three weeks before my father's death, something strange happens to me, not directly connected with him. I'm walking down Shipka Street one late afternoon, under the unseasonably merciful November sun. A young woman coming up the pavement towards me smiles and stops me. *Aren't you . . .? Yes, I am. Your books saved me; do you have five minutes for a coffee?*

I reply that I'm in a bit of a hurry, which is the truth. She looks at me and makes a comment in such a normal and even tone that at first I think I've misheard her.

I want to kill myself, she says again, realising that I haven't grasped what she said.

It comes like a slow punch to the stomach. Indeed, everything about this encounter is in slow motion, especially my reactions. I look around helplessly. A few last yellow leaves are gently falling around us, a group of noisy students are heading towards the university, my father is on his deathbed at home . . . The first thing that crosses my mind to say is – Me, too. I swallow it back. But the girl is standing in front of me, looking at me with such expectation, sure that I will pull out some words of consolation and meaning, like a magician pulling a rabbit out of a hat.

Let's see what you're really made of, since you love to write about meaning and consolation.

What do you mean, you want to kill yourself, there's no point, I say, playing for time.

That's not the worst of it, she says, glancing down, *I'm pregnant and nobody wants this kid. They're trying to force me into the psych ward.*

I don't remember what I said. Most likely all the banal bullshit one says in such instances, taken mainly from cheap self-help books and Hollywood movies. *You've got to hold on for the child's sake. Go back to your parents, talk to them, they'll understand. They'll understand, I'm sure they will, parents always do.*

They don't even want to hear about it, she answers evenly. The whole time – and this is what strikes me as the scariest part – the girl speaks with the absolute calm of a person who has made a decision. With such overriding calm, devoid of posturing, devoid of hysteria, she simply states it like a person telling a friend she is thinking about going to the movies.

If you kill yourself, you'll become a killer, too, I say, *and you're not a killer. Just talk to the child. Go in, listen to it and decide together.*

I give her my phone number in case there's any way I can help, and we go our separate ways.

71

My father's things, which were left behind and which I kept, this tiny museum of everyday life, a museum for an unheroic person: a cork cigarette lighter, which I had brought him from Lisbon just a few weeks earlier; a pack of blue Rothmans with three cigarettes left inside, he had last lit up two in bed and taken only a few drags, just enough to re-enact the gesture, to feel that he was still alive; the final newspapers with crossword puzzles he had solved; a Swiss Army knife; his glasses with an outdated prescription (he was always meaning to get new ones, but only after all his work was done, which was never) and old-fashioned, thick, horn-rimmed frames, which had come back into fashion in the meantime. And the walking stick he came with, handmade from dogwood or beech more than thirty years ago, thanks to a torn meniscus.

A friend was telling me how, when his father died, he hadn't felt any particular sadness and was even a bit worried about himself. A week passed, then a month, and he felt nothing out of the ordinary; of course, he thought about him, he wasn't cheerful, but actual sadness – nope. *Then one morning*, he told me, *I opened my eyes and I couldn't get up from the grief, I'm telling you. It was as if some heavy slab of stone was pressing down on my chest, I couldn't catch my breath, it just struck me all of a sudden, as if I only then realised that my father was gone. It took me till the next year to start feeling better,* he said.

A few more things from my father's legacy:

His new shoes (that had once been mine), which he would wear when he went into town. They disappeared somehow, thanks to the funeral directors. His leather jacket, which he had bought only a month before coming to Sofia and which he still couldn't get enough of, also disappeared in the same way. His wallet, now scuffed, a present from my brother; inside it there are small, folded-up scraps of paper with the phone numbers of his nearest and dearest. I remember how seventeen years ago, when he realised death lurked nearby, he stuffed a little calendar with the icon of St George into his wallet, along with photos of his two grandchildren as little kids. Now I did not find those guardian angels of his. He hadn't been able to prepare himself, everything happened so fast.

Add to this a few leftover opioid patches, as well as the folder of medical documents and test results, plus his little photo album from college, and this exhausts the list of things he had around him in his final days. There was something ascetic and beautiful in how few possessions my father required. His entire estate and legacy was growing in the garden. He didn't need anything else – he was content to wear our hand-me-down clothes. He would get angry if we spent our money buying him something new for the holidays. *When will I ever wear them*, he would say again and again, *I'm not gonna live forever with the eagles . . .*

And he left something more: words of his that I keep and which turn up at unexpected moments, that run through my mind for days on end. *'Tihnaluk'*, or siletude, is one of the nicest. *C'mere*, he'd tell me, *and sit a while in siletude*. In *tih-na-luk*, somewhere between silence and solitude, such a quiet word that it even flickers slightly. It can usually be sensed at sundown, at twilight, when even the silence is translucent, and the birds stop singing for a moment. *C'mere*, he said, *and sit for a bit in tihnaluk*.

Now I'm sitting here in siletude, in a different place, far from my father, speaking with him.

I remember the way he'd pronounce certain words, sometimes deliberately, other times out of habit – *clouthes*, instead of clothes, as if he were putting on clouds, *zweet* instead of sweet, which leaves a stronger phonetic sweetness on the palate . . .

I remember how my father yawned before going to bed. (That yawn made it into a story as well, part of the golden collection of must-hear things before I go completely deaf.)

I remember the way he smoked, the bluish smoke would make fleeting figures that faded into the air.

I remember how he pursed his lips when he was angry or upset.

I remember how he would sink into the garden, dragging his legs at the end, bent over, wearing my old red jacket. And how for a moment, I saw myself as him.

72

The beginning of that poem by W.H. Auden 'In Memory of W.B. Yeats', will always carry me off towards my father.

He disappeared in the dead of winter:
The brooks were frozen, the airports almost deserted,
And snow disfigured the public statues;
The mercury sank in the mouth of the dying day.

That last line especially makes me shudder.

I never saw my father reading poetry. But precise phrases from various poems remind me of him now.

Something from William Carlos Williams's 'The Red Wheelbarrow' too:

so much depends
upon

a red wheel
barrow

glazed with rain
water

Perhaps because we had just such a wheelbarrow in the yard, leaning up against the wall, slightly rusty, with chickens always circling around it. Actually, now that I think about it, he knew quite a few poems by heart, most often those that were not part of the canon. I never asked him where he'd learned them. He also knew by heart all the terrible poems I'd written as a child. I only realised this in his final years.

73

In the days that followed his death, I spend whole afternoons playing chess on the computer so as not to think.
It doesn't work. My father finds a way to sneak into the
game; he even gives me a sour look when I make a wrong
move. I start playing speed chess, three minutes a game,
so not a single empty second is left for thinking. Again, it
doesn't work. He was the one who taught me.

My father taught me to play chess. At first, he would
play without a queen, to more or less even things up. This
didn't help me much. Once I got a bit better, he'd keep
his queen but get rid of one of the lesser figures, say a
rook. Then many years passed when I didn't play chess
with him at all. Some time ago, we sat down to play again.
On that same wooden chess board from my childhood
(the knight was still missing a head). He'd been given it
by a friend when he was young, and the phrase 'May you
always be victorious!' was pyrogravured into the inside.
And he was. That time, however, I won, perhaps for the
first time. I couldn't believe it. Neither could he. *If you
want, I can play without my queen*, I said in his voice from

forty years ago. Smack-talking was part of the game, and he was also the king of that, he's the one I learned it from.

74

Yet again, that unlocking of sorrow by specific little things.
The mandarin orange I pick up and then suddenly realise that it was the last fruit he ate a piece of, with so
much agony, before ceasing to eat entirely. A mandarin is
no longer simply a mandarin.

Sometimes I forget he's gone, and it's a happy moment; I
pick up the phone to call him and then it hits me.

I notice that the same adverts are playing on TV – the
ones he liked and the ones that drove him crazy. (The unbearable immortality of commercialised being.)
    I saved the last newspapers I had bought for him. So
I would know what kind of world he left behind. A war
in Europe, yet another in Palestine, angry arguments for
and against getting rid of the Soviet Army Monument
in downtown Sofia, yet more scandals . . . To know what
kind of world he left us in.

*

The final days of December run out. Sharp absence around
seven in the evening. In two days it'll be New Year. The
holidays are an especially difficult time for grief. Adverts

about getting together with your nearest and dearest beam from the television, grinning Santa Clauses hug children, the whole extended family is in the living room, and the father cuts an endless sausage into impossibly thin slices. *Enjoy the holidays*, they wish me at the shop.

Doctor, can I at least hope to get together with the kids at Christmas?

The doctor hesitates for three treacherous seconds before saying – *Yes, for Christmas you can.*

75

My father didn't really love me, a friend of mine says. This is to some extent a feeling shared by our whole generation. Our fathers didn't spoil us, that much is true, indulgence was the purview of mothers and grandmothers. They didn't check our Bulgarian and maths homework. My father only helped out with my homework in industrial arts, when I had to make a pincushion, an iron candlestick or something ultra-practical like metal tongs for taking canning jars out of a boiling cauldron.

Actually, our fathers did love us; I'm sure of that about my father, it's just that they didn't know how to show it. No one had shown them how to do it. Only their grandchildren were able to overcome that awkward armour.

I don't remember him ever kissing me as a child. He didn't remember his father kissing him, either. Only kiss children when they're asleep, so they don't get spoiled, that's what they said in these parts. Balkan patriarchal nonsense. But my grandfather, his father, would hug us and play with us, as compensation for what had been missed. My father was truly close to my brother's son, who also played basketball. He would stay up whole nights, buy tickets and travel all over with his grandson's college team. The boys loved him, he was their talisman. Fifty years later, his dream of being on the basketball court was coming true, albeit in a different body.

My father adored my daughter, he spoiled her, indulged her, obeyed her every whim. He had made her a little child-sized hoe, and they would dig in the garden together. Once he tried skipping because she asked him to, and came crashing down onto the cement. Thank God he didn't break anything. We were doubled over with laughter, my daughter most of all, while he got up, dusted himself off sheepishly and said like a little kid – *It's OK, I'm fine, I'm not hurt, there's nothing to fear.*

76

Only now do I realise how important they were to me as a child – all his, albeit meagre, signs of . . . I'm not sure what the right word is. Praise, for example: him praising me for something. It didn't happen often. Which is why I remember every one of those (two or three) times.

Once was during those rare moments when the three of us – my brother, my father and I – were looking through some magazine together, most likely *Cosmos* or one of those scarce copies of *Parallels* that we had somehow got a hold of. There was a game 'Discover the Difference' between two identical pictures. Together we'd found eight of them, but for the life of us we could not find the ninth. Then I happened to spot it. *Bravo, that was the hardest one*, my father said. It was forty-five years ago, but I haven't forgotten it.

Thinking back on it now, as I child I was hardly what he would have imagined as the ideal son. I was shy and withdrawn, constantly reading and secretly writing (which meant that everybody knew about it). I never got into fights with other boys except for once, and with a kid who was older than me at that, an incident which I believe very much surprised my father and made me rise in his estimation.

The truth is that after my brother and I left to do our mandatory military service and then went to Sofia, during every visit home over the years, we would hug him for a little longer upon our arrival. We extended the alibi of greeting and sending off guests to conceal an ever-longer embrace.

When I had to report for army service, my father drove me in his Polish Fiat to that distant northern town I'd been assigned to. My head was shaved, which made me look even more scrawny and gangly than usual, the military uniform the officer tossed to me hung off me like hand-me-downs. I saw my father's eyes filling with tears, he turned and spent a long moment blowing his nose in his handkerchief. That's how our fathers wept when they were younger. I'm not sure if we hugged then.

I recalled my grandma telling a story about how when the family got word that the soldiers were coming back from the front after the Second World War, they went to the train station in S. to wait for my grandfather. They stayed there for several days, sleeping in their carts. When that long-awaited train finally arrived, my grandfather appeared at the door, alive and well after nine months at war. *I felt like running up to him, hugging him and not letting him go,* my grandma said . . . *but my father-in-law shot me a look and said – Hold your horses, young bride. And in the end, when my turn came, I just held out my hand to your grandfather and he shook it: he, too, didn't dare embrace me in front of his father. What fools we were,* my grandma said, wiping her eyes with the edge of her headscarf.

77

Several months after my father's death, I ran into a Bulgarian artist who had long ago emigrated to Italy. *You know what*, he said, lighting up as he saw me, *we ran into each other briefly years ago, you probably don't remember, it was at the seaside in Sozopol, but you said something then that changed my life, as they say. I used that line of yours, but rest assured I quoted you*, he hurried to add, *and made it into the best exhibition I've had so far.*

And what was that line? I asked, curious.

Well, I told you that I was an emigrant who still felt anchored here, in Bulgaria, and you replied, just like that, off the cuff – *While my anchor grows ever lighter . . .*

The whole afternoon that phrase runs through my head. *While my anchor grows ever lighter.* Words find us when they need to. I said something without thinking much of it, perhaps just because of the phrase itself, and only now, after my father's death, does it fill with meaning. But this does not make me grow lighter.

78

This'll be a long sorrow, a friend says. It's a pretty phrase, but I'm still deep in the midst of the pain.First comes a long pain. The sorrow comes after . . .

I try to localise that pain in my body, to pinpoint where exactly it's springing from. Now it's low in my chest, where the diaphragm is, needling me, preventing me from catching my breath. Actually, the pain is migratory. Now it's up in my throat, somewhere there, where the centre of sobbing is. Now it's doughy, like under-baked bread, difficult to swallow.

The notebook I'm writing in was started in October. This means that when it began, my father was still alive. Only thirty pages ago, he was still alive. And no one had any idea of what would follow.

In one of his early essays, 'Of Sorrow', Montaigne describes how great grief paralyses and petrifies a person. Thus Niobe, having lost her seven sons and seven daughters, turned to stone, transformed into a cliff, as Ovid tells us. Sorrow moves beyond words.

He who can describe how his heart is ablaze is burning on a small pyre, Petrarch writes in one of his sonnets.

Yes, this is likely a small fire of grief, since you can speak, write, string together words. I only wonder whether the kindling of those words cool it, or just inflame it all the more.

Again Montaigne, this time in one of his late essays, 'Of the Resemblance of Children to Their Fathers'. He begins by complaining about kidney stones, the affliction he was most afraid of and from which his father died in terrible agony. Here he reflects upon pain and fear of death in a much more personal way. *So much are men enslaved to their miserable being, that there is no condition so wretched they will not accept, provided they may live!*

Words spoken, I now suspect, before the real pain arrived.

79

My father, of course, did not know the consolations of philosophy, nor did he wrack his brains over how to learn to accept death; he did not page through Zenon and Seneca, nor did he get up and lie down with Marcus Aurelius, yet this did not prevent him from being a stoic, a naive Naturphilosoph, believing in virtue and nature. Even though he was not familiar with Pseudo-Longinus or Kant, he could still recognise the sublime and cast an eye towards the starry heavens above us. I will allow myself to present here as evidence that story about buffalo shit, told in another novel of mine, which takes us back from the realm of fiction into reality, where this story, in fact, belongs. It tells how, when all of us were in awe over the architecture and cherrywood cannon of an open-air museum town, my father stopped on the street for a long time, hovering over something on the ground.

I went to see what he had discovered. A pile of buffalo shit. It was standing there like a miniature cathedral, a church's cupola or a mosque's dome, may all religions forgive me. A fly was circling above it like an angel. It is very rare to see buffalo shit nowadays, my father said. No one breeds buffaloes here any more. And he spoke with such delight about how one could fertilise pumpkins with it, plaster a wall, daub a beehive (of the old wicker type), how one could use it to cure an earache – you should warm it well and apply it to the ear. At that moment I would have agreed that the Revival-Era houses we were touring and the Pyramids of Giza were something much less important than the architecture, physics and metaphysics of buffalo (bull?) shit. Even if you weren't born in Versailles, Athens, Rome or Paris, the sublime will always find a form in which to appear before you.

If I ever belong to a school of thought, I would like that to be my father's invisible school, according to which you can see the sublime in a pile of buffalo shit. *The sublime is everywhere.*

80

He's everywhere in your books, a friend says. *He's the real storyteller in your family*, my wife needles me. One of the stories I remember from my childhood, as told in his inimitable way with all his self-deprecation, was about how he would surreptitiously hang out the laundry on my mother's orders at night, so that no one would see him and he wouldn't become a laughing stock, the butt of local jokes. At that time, it must've been the seventies, hanging out the laundry, just like washing the clothes themselves, was considered pure women's work. *So I slink out at night in my undershirt, to the cats' horror, and hang out the laundry in the yard*, my father would say, *but as bad luck would have it, the neighbour is out smoking, so he calls to me through the fence, he's a serious fellow, getting on in years, one of the old bourgeoisie.* So my father was caught with his pants down, as it were, while hanging out his wife's underpants. He could make anything into a story, even the laundry.

I put all this into a story, complete with all his exaggeration and irony, and entitled it 'Catching History with Its Pants Down'. And when the story came out, again as bad luck would have it, his friends got wind of it (I say 'bad luck', because generally they weren't big on reading). They read it or someone retold it to them, and then they started calling him up on the phone to give him a hard time. *Damn, but they busted my balls over that*, my father would complain, wagging a scolding finger at me. *I put you in a story*, I would tell him, *you should be a little more grateful. OK fine, you put me in a story, but with my pants down*, he would reply.

But worse yet was ending up in one of *his* stories; we all fell victim to that.

Laid to rest along with him is the story about my mother and my aunt's first unsuccessful attempts to make a *pantespani* sponge cake, which according to the recipe was supposed to be slightly springy. About how they burned it and then threw it out for the chickens, but even they didn't want to eat it and ran away in a panic, because when they pecked at the cake, it popped back up at them. Only the cockerel battled it to the bitter end.

Or about the first pancakes he and my mother decided to make, when they had just moved to the city. They ran over to ask the neighbour, Granny Penka. *Is the batter OK, Granny Penka? Hmm, looks a little watery to me, add some more flour. So I run down to the shop*, my father would say, *and buy three packages of flour, dump them in the batter and head back over to Granny Penka's. Oh dear*, she said, clutching her head in her hands, *now you've made it too thick, dagnabbit, are you gonna bake bricks or what? Add some more water.* So I pour in water straight from the hose (here my father really let his imagination run wild). In the end, they had so much batter that they cooked waffles all day long.

Then my father went down to the street, and fortunately kids were passing by on their way home from the nearby school, so he shoved a pancake in every kid's hand. *Four whole classes passed by, and we still had two buckets of pancakes left over*, he would end the story with a flourish.

My mother, who had already heard these stories a hundred times, would get irritated and snap – *Just look at him, exaggerating like that. OK fine, so it was three whole classes and one bucket of leftovers*, my father would agree, to keep the peace.

81

Several years ago, we went together to visit that house, the happiest home of my childhood, the one with the yard in the town of T., and it seemed to have shrunk dramatically. The enormous wooden gate had been reduced to a narrow metal door, while the window where I would spend my afternoons was absolutely tiny, shabby and cracked. But the biggest metamorphosis was what had happened to the garden – that yard with the giant cherry tree, which we'd climbed to peek at the cards of the old men playing bridge beneath it or to peer into our neighbour Blind Mariyka's yard . . . The cherry tree had dried up and now jutted up like a mere monument to itself and our long-ago childhood. The fig tree next to the outhouse at the other end of the yard was also desiccated, while the flower beds with my father's famous Dutch tulips, which he carried with him everywhere, had shrunk to the sizes of handkerchiefs. I am convinced a child's eye has the ability to expand space. When you are as tall as roses and tulips, you look at the world up close, you are at its eye level, and it's at yours.

Growing up distances and diminishes.

*

Our family life from that time could be described through our migrations from one rented apartment to the next, always on the ground floor or the basement, because they were cheaper.

Our first apartment was the one in the town of T., with the cherry tree, with a single window looking right out onto the pavement, with a wide sill inside, upon which I spent my late afternoons, eight years old and alone, my fears growing ever stronger, moving at the speed of the falling twilight. When my mother and father were late getting home, a slight sense of abandonment would creep in.

Anyway, in that house on the street with the strange name of Sergienko – which they tell me is still there on the road signs – the four of us lived in a single basement room. I recall that in the beginning, there was only one bed, which my brother and I slept in, while my mother and father slept on the floor. But suddenly, after the cat had her kittens on their blanket, my mother found the whole arrangement gruesome, so they borrowed money and bought a second bed. Which left only enough space in the room for a table and an oil-burning stove. (Ubiquitous at the time, those oil-burning stoves sometimes exploded like bombs, or at least so went the rumours.) But even then that room seemed spacious to me. Everything happened in it. Since there was no other room, my brother and I were allowed to hear the adults' furtive conversations while we pretended to be asleep in bed. What were those conversations about? I've forgotten now, but we knew that whatever was spoken there should not be repeated to anyone, especially what was said in quiet, low murmurs. Once, when we had guests over, we couldn't help ourselves and burst out laughing at some joke, one of those told in a whisper. The guests were worried, but my father merely turned to us and said: *You know, don't you?*

Of course we know, it goes without saying.

Once I asked my mother and father whether we were poor. We had just come back from visiting some friends of ours, whose kids went to the same school as us. That family lived in their own spacious apartment, they had enormous, plush armchairs, in their glass cabinets stood a souvenir Venetian gondola, and a winking postcard in front of it. The daughter, who was in my class, kept her pens in an empty can of Coca Cola, and her eraser smelled like strawberry. Having nothing became shameful primarily in comparison to someone else having something.

In response to my question *are we poor?*, I received only silence from my father, who was lighting up a cigarette, and a huffy reply from my mother that there was no longer any such thing as 'rich' or 'poor'.

82

We had a family friend, an engineer, who found himself in West Germany for three days, on a business trip. *He was probably there for industrial espionage*, my father never failed to add. So this guy went into a German bakery and said from the doorway: *A loaf of bread, please*, the saleswoman shrugged and pointed to the racks behind her, which held not simply (one kind of) bread, but all the breads of the world – sliced, whole, white, yellow, brown, whole-wheat, cornbread, rye . . . Our man was used to plain white bread, factory-made. He stared at that enormous abundance of bread and names, and couldn't decide: he had no idea what exactly he wanted, nor what it was called. He felt such a deep sense of shame that he realised he was on the brink of bursting into tears, so he turned on his heel and ran out of the bakery as fast as he could.

Somewhere in *Demons*, I think it is, Dostoevsky says that a person is unhappy because he doesn't know that he is happy, that's the only reason. My father, who could never be accused of reading too much Dostoevsky, argued the exact opposite. I heard him once telling a group of friends in a slightly hushed voice (perhaps that's why I remember it): *Here, we're happy only because we don't know how unhappy we are.* Of course, this was a purely political statement. And that isolation, that other world which was denied to us, even as a basis for comparison, worked to the advantage of our 'happiness'.

83

We later moved to the larger town of Y., but the apartment we rented there was almost identical, on the ground floor, a semi-basement, from where you could only see cats and people's shoes, and with no yard to boot. It was the very beginning of the eighties. The first half of that decade will always remain subterranean for me, scented with mustiness and moisture.

Several years later, we were given a larger apartment on an upper floor for the first time, thanks to my mother's job. Suddenly sunlight entered the rooms, the world grew brighter, we no longer looked at everything from below like Minotaurs. Unfortunately, we had to leave that place too, two or three years later. At that time my mother and father were finally given the right to buy an apartment, on the outskirts of town naturally, so we moved into our own apartment, which they spent years paying off. And that was the last place we lived together as a family, in my late teenage years, before I did my army service and then left for Sofia.

That was the story of our life together in brief, told through various moves between cities and apartments. In ascending order, nevertheless – from the basement to the seventh floor.

And so one of my father's late bourgeois dreams came true of having his own apartment, in a modern building, of sitting in an armchair, grabbing a newspaper and putting his feet up on a footstool. But when that dream finally became reality, after all those peregrinations, he held out for only three or four years before he began complaining that there wasn't any fresh air there, he wanted to go out into a yard, but there wasn't one. And so he went back to the village to look after his elderly father, who was still tirelessly working in the garden.

In his final days, I innocently tried to strike up conversations about our early years, the yard outside our first apartment, which was covered in red leaves every autumn. Our car trips to the seaside in our Polish Fiat (it's a Fiat, but a Polish one, it's Polish, but still a Fiat, as we liked to smack-talk in the neighbourhood). Getting to the seaside was a true odyssey, even though we lived just a stone's throw from the coast, some negligible eighty or ninety kilometres. How can I conjure now the ritual of departing early in the morning while it was still dark, the hard-boiled eggs and *lyutenitsa* that we'd eat beside a roadside fountain halfway through the journey while we waited for the car to cool down, followed by a round of vomiting by me and my brother, and then there we were, practically at the seaside.

And let's not forget the game of who would be the first to spot the sea around a bend, our pleas to go swimming that very same day, pitching the tent, the requisite first holiday quarrel between my mother and father . . .

My father was a sort of Atlas, holding the past on his shoulders. Now that he is gone, I can sense that whole past cracking, quietly collapsing in on me, burying me in all its afternoons. The quietly collapsing afternoons of childhood. And there is no one I can call to for help.

84

Once again in those final days, he and I are looking at photos together. The archive is minuscule, of course, we have no culture of that kind of record-keeping here. Just a few torn and faded documents. My great-grandmother's marriage certificate. A photo of a field hospital with a hole in the middle, showing my great-grandfather, wounded in the Balkan War. My grandfather's baptismal certificate and three or four of his letters from the front in the Second World War, in handwriting that is no longer legible.

If I am the archivist, then my father is the living history of the family. *Ask him who that is, he knows them all*, our relatives would say. That unwritten family history is now gone. I know that with my father's death, not just one, but several worlds disappeared.

My father endeavoured to look after all those past worlds with their complex ecosystems. *At night, when I couldn't sleep*, he would say, *I go through them in my head, listing off all the folks from the village who've passed away in the last fifteen years, how many houses are left. I organise them by neighbourhoods, then by families.* And he would start saying his endless rosary – *the Daskalovs, the Pisarovs, the Minnows, the Kaseryovs, the Zografs, the Tightlipped-Dimitrovs, the Snakes, Sweet Diko, Diko the Cockerel, Tsanyo the Pointer, the Little Peppers* . . .

What's more, the villagers took on the names of all their forefathers, starting with the first known ancestor in their family line, then going back as far as two centuries. My father, for example, was Nedyalko-Rus-Kolyo-Dinyov-Gergev-Dinyo. Family trees were oral in these parts, given the lack of any written ones. Through this repetition of names, generation after generation, the earliest ancestor was remembered, in this case Nedyalko, a master house-builder, who came from somewhere around Troyan in the Balkan Mountains, to work with other masons here in the south and stayed. It was the end of the eighteenth century. That's all we know about him. A single name.

My father kept these worlds alive, listing them off in his head at night, silently repeating the complex rosary of names for each family, gathering them around himself, even calling out the names of some of the more important animals. In that latter group lived Kyorcho the horse, blind but intelligent and gentle. An old she-buffalo languished there as well, whose gaze was all too human. Next to her snorted the donkey Penka, whom even I remember, my personal comrade and age-mate, the same animal my grandfather sold for three hundred leva so we could buy our first cassette player on the black market, a Hitachi mono, again from the Vietnamese. This, too, entered into the pages of our family folklore, this exchange of a donkey for a cassette player, like the folk tale where a fool trades a horse for a chicken.

*

I think perhaps this was my father's mission, though he did not know it: to serve as the shepherd of a small flock of stories, which he raised himself and which followed him around everywhere at his heels. Or simply to be a gardener – there in the garden of stories and family trees.

85

. . . there are more dreamed people than us. / But
they don't take up any space . . .

*– Tomas Tranströmer in a poem entitled
'Dream Seminar'*

There are also more dead people than there are us, I think
when I read those lines. And even though they don't
take up any space, they settle into other rooms, they pass
through other invisible doors in time, where we briefly
cross paths with them. *Yesterday's rooms*, as Gaustine would
say, *afternoon rooms, with dim light and a dead butterfly in
the ashtray on the table. You need to step lightly there*, he would
always instruct me, *so you don't disturb the dust, and remember to shut the door nice and firmly so the times don't mix.*
And don't touch the clock, it's right in another time . . .

*

As I write this, a heavy, constricting sorrow washes over
me once again. It's three in the afternoon. Afternoons will
no longer be the same.

I keep taking photos of wilting flowers, in various stages

of drooping, fading, of their falling petals, starkly exposed pistil and stamens, already senescent, having outlived their seductive function. Blighted and dying flowers . . . There is a strange sorrow and beauty in their wilting, without the despair that accompanies the ageing of people and animals. This is surely the reason I continue to snap pictures of dying roses, periwinkles, tulips, balding peonies, dwindling calla lilies and violets . . . Botany knows how to die beautifully, without really dying. Botany still knows more about death.

86

I see him, I see us walking together along the shore of the sea early in the morning, before dawn. I'm ten years old. We break into a light jog, then stop, stretch our arms and take deep breaths. The sun will show itself any moment now, the morning chill has chased away our drowsiness. What are we doing? Breathing in iodine vapours – that secret superpower of our childhood. We Bulgarians, who have no other natural resources like oil and gas, are rich in iodine vapours. However, there is no way to export them, nor is there any way to conserve them. We're always wealthy with such fleeting, meagre things.

The waves wash over our feet, the water is cold, we start running again – my father, my brother, two years younger than me, and I. We try to lengthen our strides to fit into our father's footsteps in the sand.

I'm dreaming about this episode, which did really happen, but in the dream, things start to go slightly awry. As we're running towards the cliffs at the far end of the beach, everything is fine, my father is young, we are kids. We turn around, and nothing is the same any more. My father's hair has gone white, and he starts to visibly slow down, halfway there he can barely hobble along, his legs are dragging, he's bent over. My brother and I pick up our pace to catch up with him, but the distance between us and him remains the same. Then he stops, turns towards us and makes a half-circle with his hand, while the sea, ever stronger and deeper, washes over him. We're running as fast as we can, but we're not actually moving at all, we're yelling *Daaad . . . Daaad . . .* Only the word *heeelp* comes out of my mouth.

That's how I wake up. *You were yelling something,* my daughter says.

87

Nearly four months have passed. I'm standing in the garden, it's now spring. Strange, I think to myself, my father is gone, but spring has arrived. Did I tell the roses – roses, your gardener is no longer here, but you go ahead and bloom anyway. Did I tell the cherry trees – my father is no longer here, but don't grieve, burst into flower and bear as much fruit as you can. Did I tell the roots of that which was about to sprout and bud – the one who cared for you is no longer here, but don't be afraid, isn't the heavenly gardener watching over all of us . . . or however the saying goes.

The truth was that the garden needed planting, pruning, spraying, hoeing, weeding. And I didn't know how to plant a cherry tree. Or what spray to use against aphids. Or even how far apart the tomatoes should be planted. All that solid knowledge disappeared with him. My brother and I read his black gardener's notebook and say – on this date he did such and such a thing, so I guess that means it's time.

We need to tend our own garden, Voltaire said, but I wonder whether he ever planted as much as a cucumber? We know that at least two dozen labourers and servants, led by two experienced gardeners, worked in his garden. That metaphor of his is possible thanks to them, to all real gardeners. Our pretty phrases stand upon their (stooped) shoulders.

Where was I over the past thirty years, I wonder, when my father was doing all of this? What have I been doing? Where is my garden?

88

This book has no obvious genre; it needs to create one for itself. Just as death has no genre. Nor does life. And the garden? Perhaps it's a genre unto itself, or it gathers all others into itself. An elegiac novel, a novel/memoir, or a novel/garden. It makes no difference to the botany of sorrow.

I didn't manage to write anything for a whole year after, a friend says.

Whereas for me, this is my salvation.

I imagine my father peeking over my shoulder, reading what I've written and scolding me. Don't bother with this stuff, go on and write your other books. Oh, and this part here isn't exactly right the way you've written it. That traffic cop wasn't from the neighbouring village, but from two villages over.

I see him again, just like on that November day, standing in the doorway, freshly arrived from Y. with his walking stick and leather jacket, his face gaunt, chiselled by the illness, like an aged James Dean, a rebel without a cause his whole life long.

The last few days, while I've been going back through the old photos, I found one that I had somehow missed until now. Small, black and white, with zigzagged edges. My father is around twenty, sitting on the steps of a not-yet-plastered house, resting his head in his hand in a pose taken from some film, he's wearing tight trousers tapered at the ankle, and . . . a leather jacket. Handsome, thin, with black wavy hair. I'm sure the jacket was borrowed from a friend, it's slightly too big for him, clearly put on for the photo.

And now, at the end, the two shots come together, superimposed – my father standing in the doorway with his leather jacket and walking stick, a sheepish smile on his face – *I've made a mess, I've wet myself.* While my daughter says softly – *I'm afraid.*

89

It's important to hold their hands as they're dying, I tell a friend who has also lost his father.

It's also important to let them go after that, he replied after a brief silence.

Once, in Italy, I received the gift of a story that I knew would come in handy sooner or later. A story about death and Christmas. When Marianne, the woman who told it to me, was ten years old, her mother died on Christmas day. They had just finished decorating the big Christmas tree, the Christmas cookies were waiting on the table, the record player kept spinning the same ABBA album – in short, Christmas down to the last detail. And out of the blue her mother had a massive heart attack. Instead of Santa Claus, an ambulance came, the doctors gave her shots and took her away, never to return again. She and her father were left in the empty house, not knowing what to do. They only knew that when Christmas rolled around again, they would immediately have to go elsewhere. *Because during that season, the loneliness,* Marianne said, *became so hard and crumbly, like a dried-up biscuit that you couldn't swallow.* At the very beginning of the year, her father opened up a map of the world, made his own atlas of where there was no Christmas, and booked the longest possible trip to the furthest part of Africa. And thus began their flight from Christmas, which lasted for a full ten years. They found the most far-flung destinations, slept in shacks, wandered through sands, and only came back when there was no trace of Christmas left.

One day, when her father, too, had passed away, she decided to go back to her family home. The first night she couldn't stand it and went to a hotel. Her parents' ghosts had no intention whatsoever of leaving the house. Everything was left exactly as it had been before that Christmas: the clothes, the now-faded armchairs and May bug wallpaper. Even her mother's dressing gown was still hanging in the hallway, as if she had put it there just a moment earlier. Marianne came back to the house during the day, but at night returned to the nearby hotel. Until one day she finally decided. She put on her mother's dressing gown, stood in front of the mirror, and started talking to them. *Look here, Mom and Dad, I live here now. Of course I won't chase you out of the house, but please do be quiet, I don't want you making noise at night. I'll leave the bedroom to you.* Then she took off the dressing gown, grabbed her favourite stuffed kangaroo, went back to the mirror and said to herself: *This is your home now, too, you won't be afraid of any ghosts, they're your mother and father after all.*

And she started living there.

That's a story I've been carrying around in my notebook for several years. I don't even need to dress up in my father's clothes, which are actually my old ones, nor do I need to stand in front of a mirror. I only know that when the snowdrops sprout or the first tulip opens, my father the gardener (or my father, the garden) will be there.

90

Grief is actually egocentric, grief for oneself in an abandoned world. *How will I live without* . . . But this is only part of the story, only one side of the leave-taking.

Because he, at that same time, was also taking his leave of us.

His leave-taking was surely more dramatic than ours. Can we peek into his final thoughts for a second and bear (for a second) what they contain?

How will I live (no, it's another word now), how will I die, how will I be deathing an entire eternity without all of you? Without you, without your brother, without your mother, without the grandkids, without Jacko the dog, without my rows of tomatoes, which I meant to plant but didn't get around to . . .

How will I be deathing (or have deathed) without everything that was, and worse yet, without everything that will come into being . . .

That's what the sorrow of the dying must be like.

Sorrow that feeds not only on the past, but on the future as well, especially on the future.

If it were only in the past, it would be easy – the further we receded into the days, the smaller the sorrow would appear, according to all the laws of perspective.

But sorrow has already laid its eggs in the coming days and waves at us from there.

Sorrow for the coming spring, when all that he has planted will show itself, but he won't be able to see it.

Sorrow over the fact that my daughter will graduate next year, and he won't be with us.

Sorrow for the day the great-grandchildren he so looked forward to will come along, but they won't remember him and he won't skip in front of them and make them laugh.

Sorrow for the cherry tree, which he planted two or three years ago and which will now yield its harvest for the first time.

The future is where the tree of sorrow will blossom, bear fruit and sprout ever more new branches.

Death is a cherry tree that ripens without you.

91

After my father passed, a family friend reminded me about a note I had sent her when my daughter was born. I had completely forgotten what I had written. She showed it to me, it read as follows: *R. was born. I don't know what to do.* Of course, afterwards I had sent around an ecstatic and detailed message full of news about the baby. But nevertheless *I don't know what to do.* My daughter was born, the event was extraordinary, which means that it was outside the normal order of things, outside ordinary days, it turned them upside down. And no one had ever taught me what to do as a newborn father.

I surely would've sent such a message today, if there had been anyone to send it to.
My father died. I don't know what to do.

I don't know what to do with the days and nights, I especially don't know what to do with the afternoons, that's where the sorrow lies hidden, as still as a cat, just sitting there, staring at me; as if a buffalo has flopped down in the middle of a room, leaving no way of getting around it.
I don't know what to do with the summers, they were

connected to him and my mother, to the house and the garden, I don't know what to do with all the memories that keep springing up, I don't know what to do with the past, nor with the days ahead.

I don't know what to do with my mother, who doesn't know what to do with my father's clothes and who keeps washing them every week.

I don't know what to do with Jacko the dog, who is still waiting for him and who will wait for him until the very end.

I don't know what to do with my utter ignorance of what to do in the garden, when to lime the trees, when to plant this or that, how deeply, and how often to water.

I don't know what to do with all the questions that will crop up in the future.

I don't know what to do with the stories I never asked him about and which remain untold.

I don't know what to do with the tools in the shed and the empty jars in the cellar.

I don't know what to do with this thing I'm writing, which is supposedly for him, but it's also for me and for all the fathers whose footsteps we race to catch up to.

I don't know what to do on his birthday; are such dates celebrated posthumously or is there now some other date that annihilates his birthday, say, the date of his death?

I don't know what to do for Christmas and Easter, for all upcoming holidays and for all the afternoons to come.

Epilogue

I'm writing by hand for the first time in years. After discovering that this is the only way I can write about my father. I began while I sat at his bedside, giving him pills, changing the patch with painkillers that were supposed to seep through the skin, I kept asking him about his childhood. I turned the end into words so that it would be bearable, I wanted to remember everything, because I didn't have a steel-trap mind like his, I didn't have his Socratic memory that had no need for paper and pencil . . .

I also wanted what I wrote to be fateful and light, as someone said, perhaps Nietzsche, perhaps someone else, fateful and light . . .

I hope I live till St George's Day, my father kept saying, *so we can all get together*. I finish the book on that date. It's St George's day. There's a thirteenth-century icon I love from Sinai, which shows St George without his spear, without his horse and dragon. His face is innocent, looking down and off to the side. A face of sorrow and hope.

Here, where I am, a light spring rain is falling upon green fields. A wispy fog huddles over the hill. If I wanted to, I could see my grandfather and my father wading through the waist-high grass, heading down the slope. I hear the invisible bells of cows and sheep. Somewhere, hidden in the trees, a cuckoo bird calls, fateful and light. *There's nothing to fear.*

6 May, St George's Day, 2024
Montricher

Acknowledgements

[to come]

Credits

Page XX – *Moral Letters to Lucilius* (Letter 24), translated by Richard M. Gummere.
Page XX – All translations from *The Iliad* are by Emily Wilson.
Page XX – Translated into English by Patty Crane.